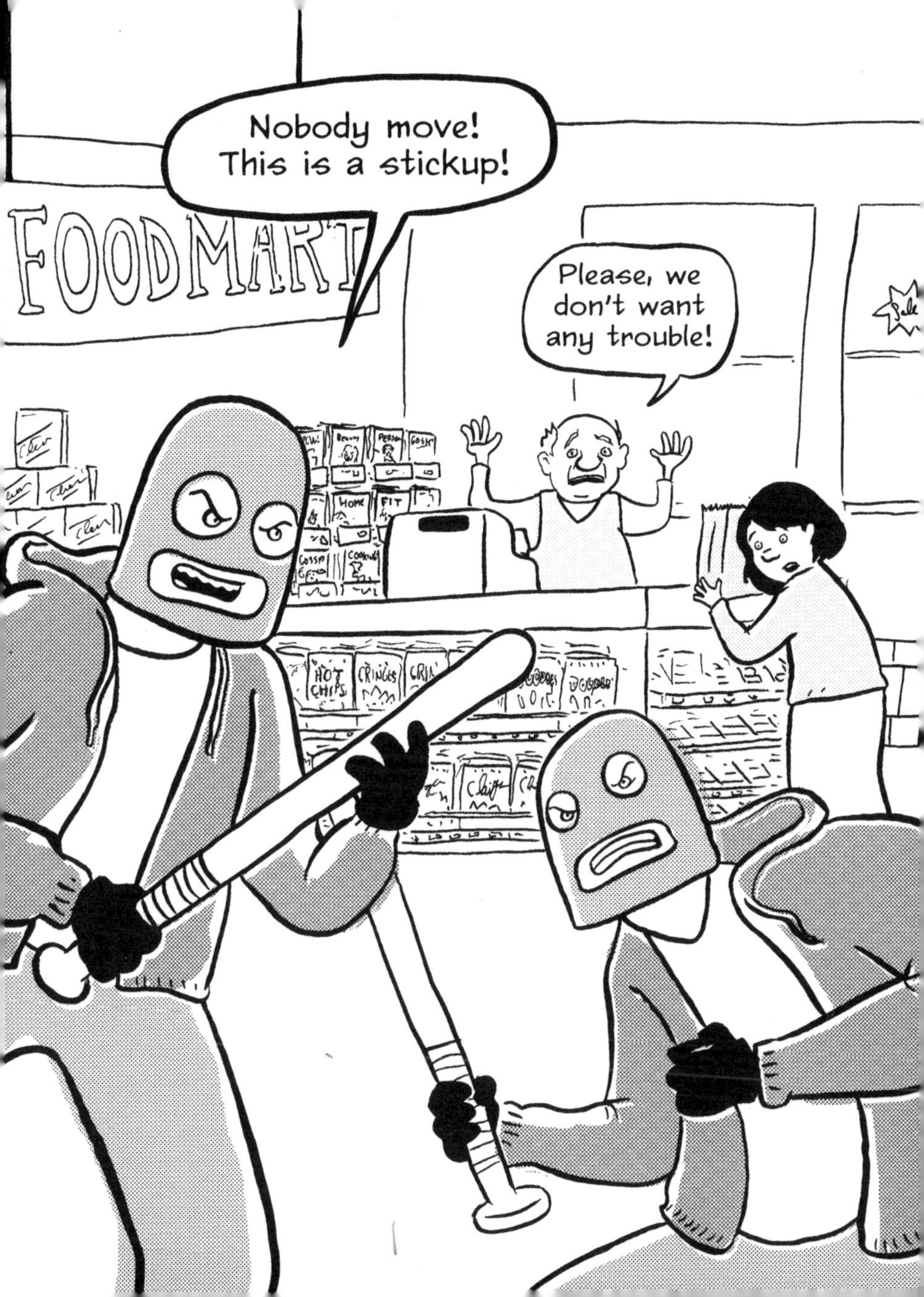
Nobody move! This is a stickup!
FOODMART
Please, we don't want any trouble!

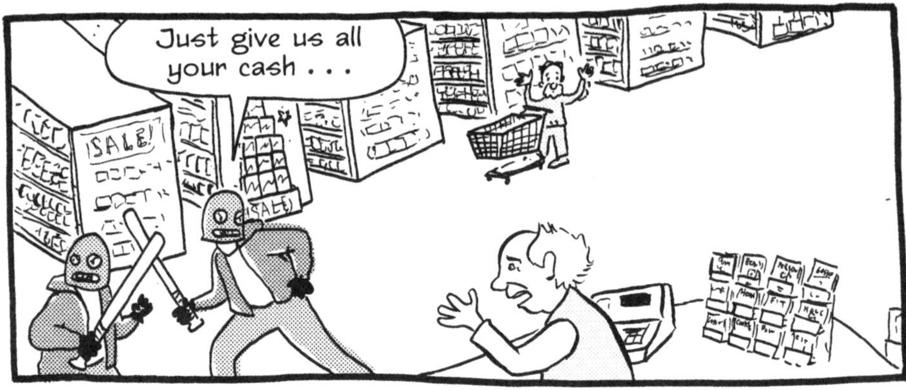
Just give us all your cash . . .
SALE!

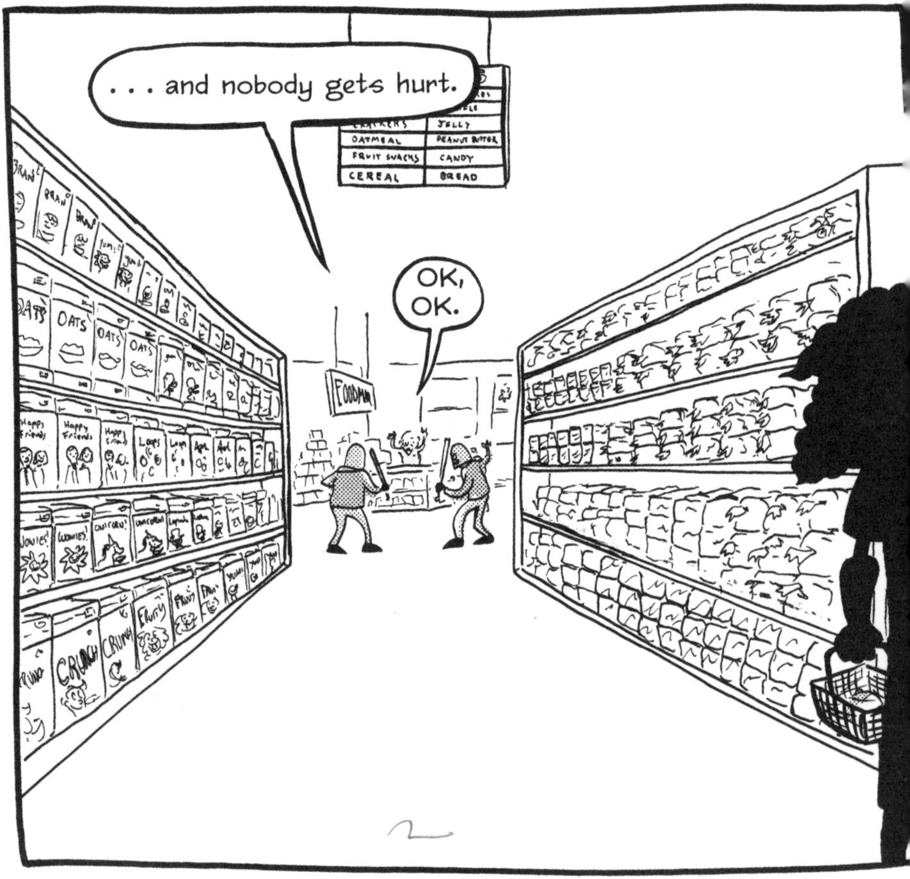
. . . and nobody gets hurt.
CRACKERS
JELLY
OATMEAL
PEANUT BUTTER
FRUIT SNACKS
CANDY
CEREAL
BREAD
OK, OK.

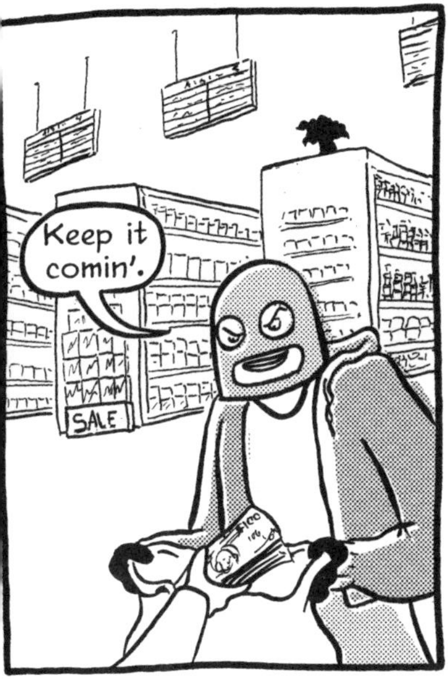
Keep it comin'.
SALE

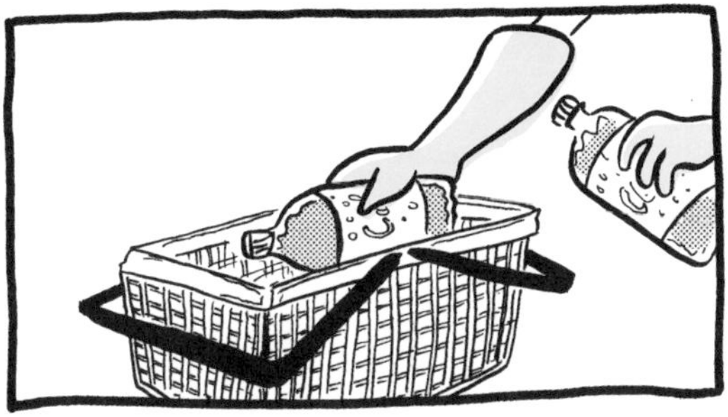

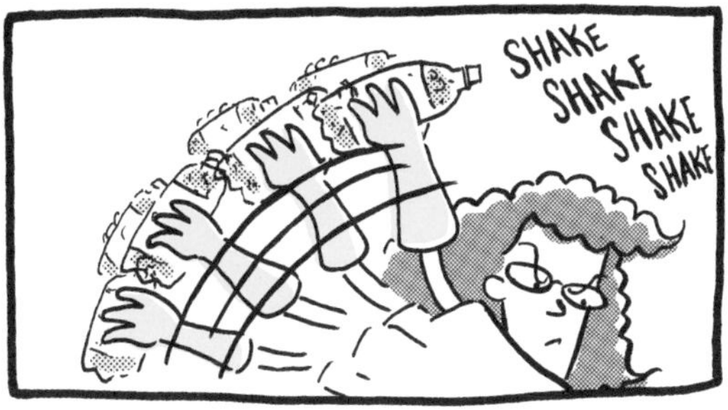
SHAKE
SHAKE
SHAKE
SHAKE

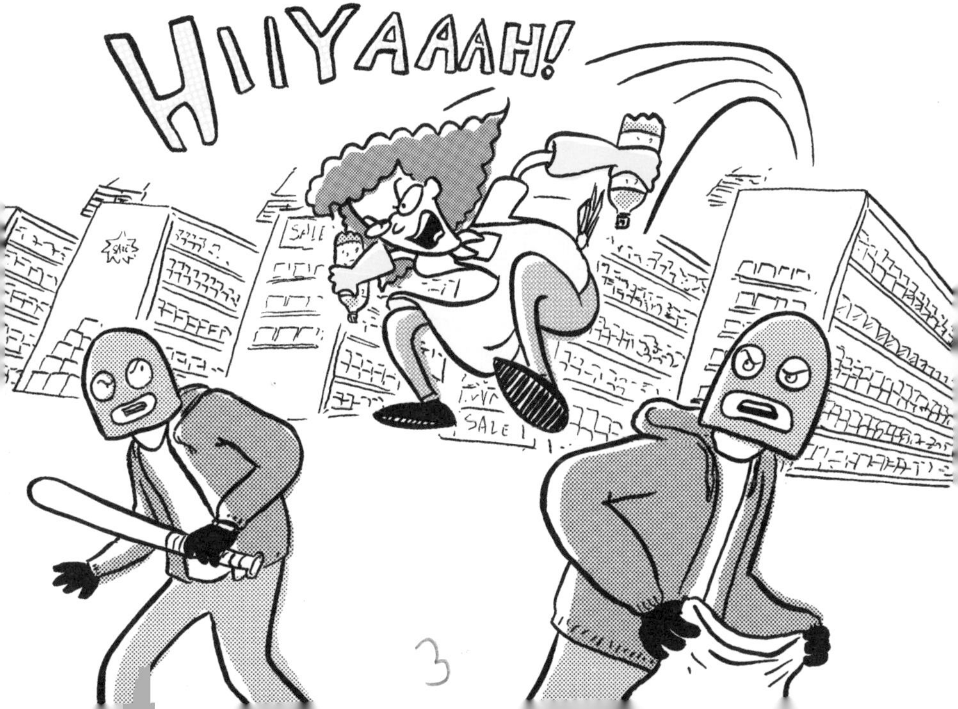
HIIYAAAH!
SALE
SALE

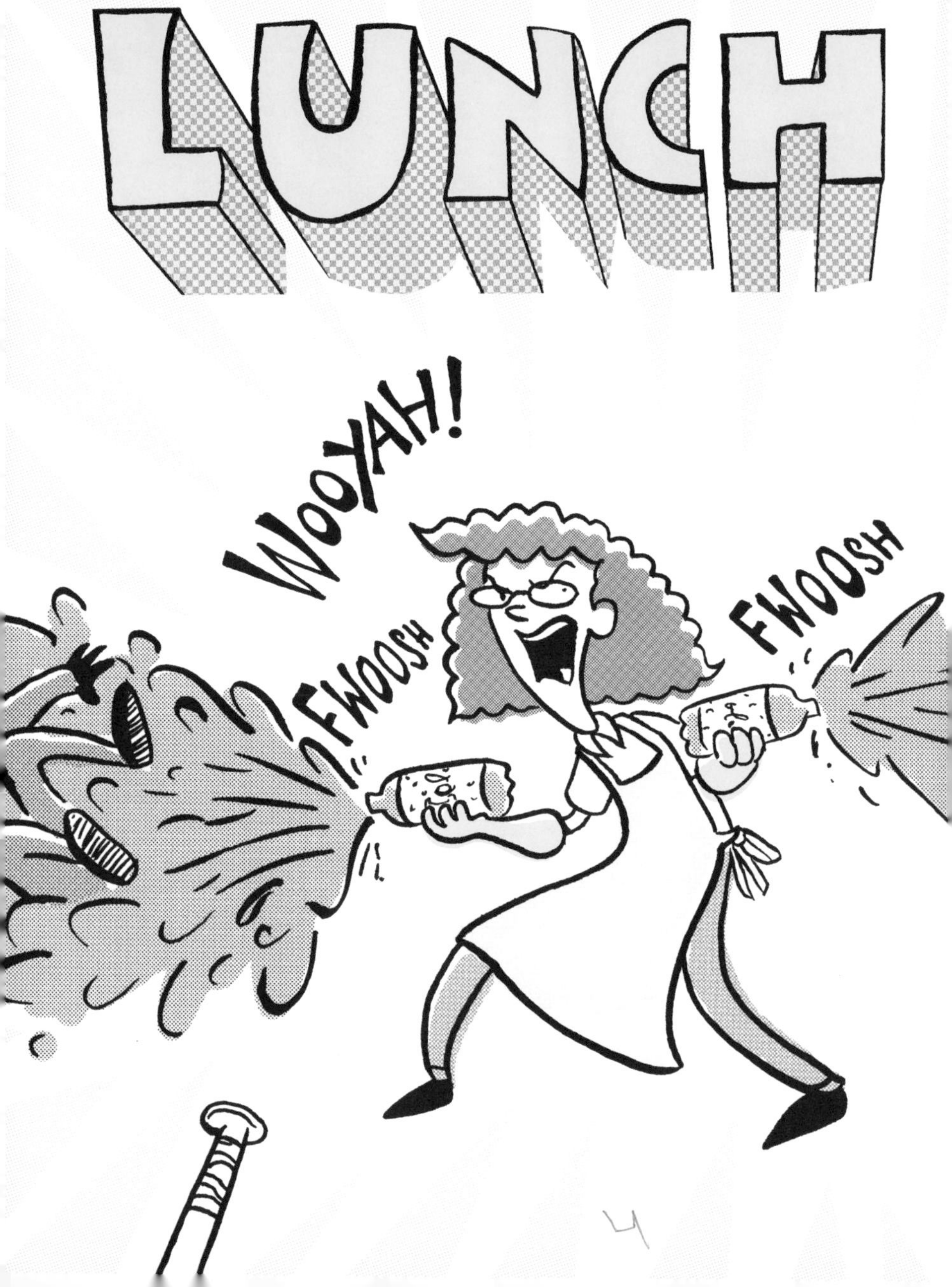
LUNCH
WOOYAH!
FWOOSH
FWOOSH
4

LADY

and the Field Trip Fiasco

Jarrett J. Krosoczka

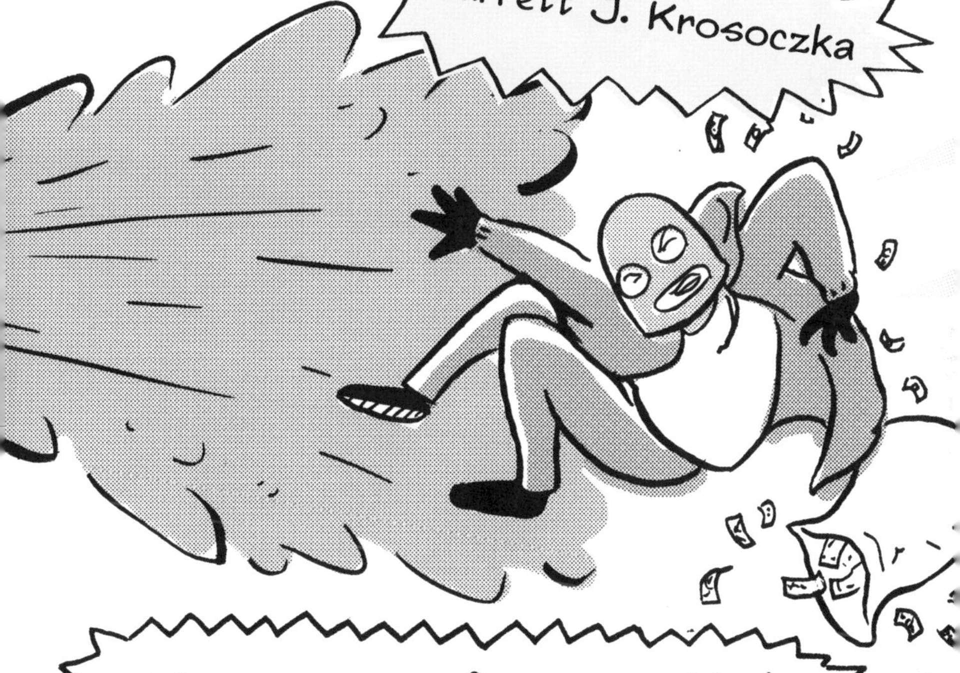

Alfred A. Knopf New York

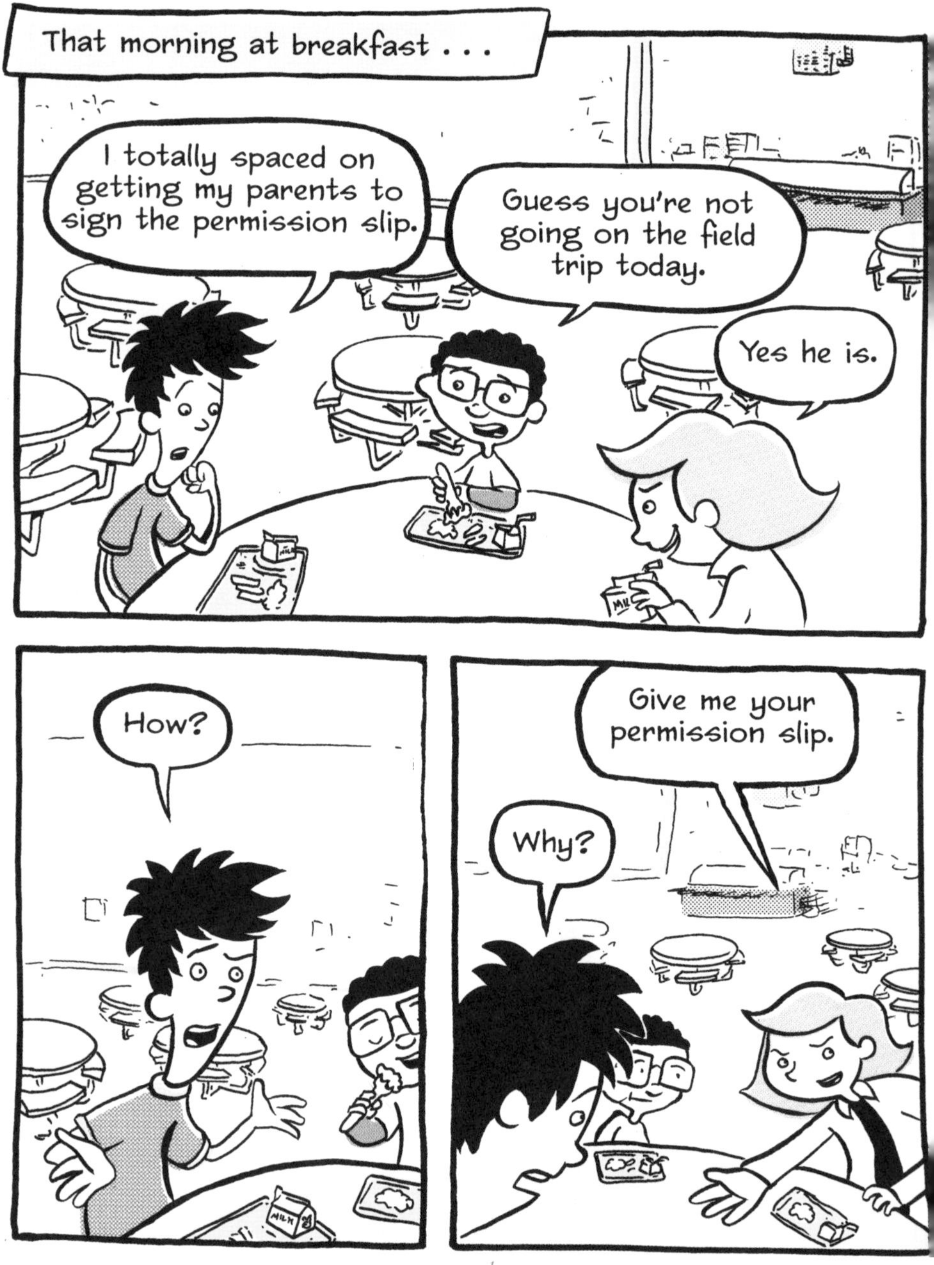

That morning at breakfast . . .
I totally spaced on getting my parents to sign the permission slip.
Guess you're not going on the field trip today.
Yes he is.
How?
Give me your permission slip.
Why?

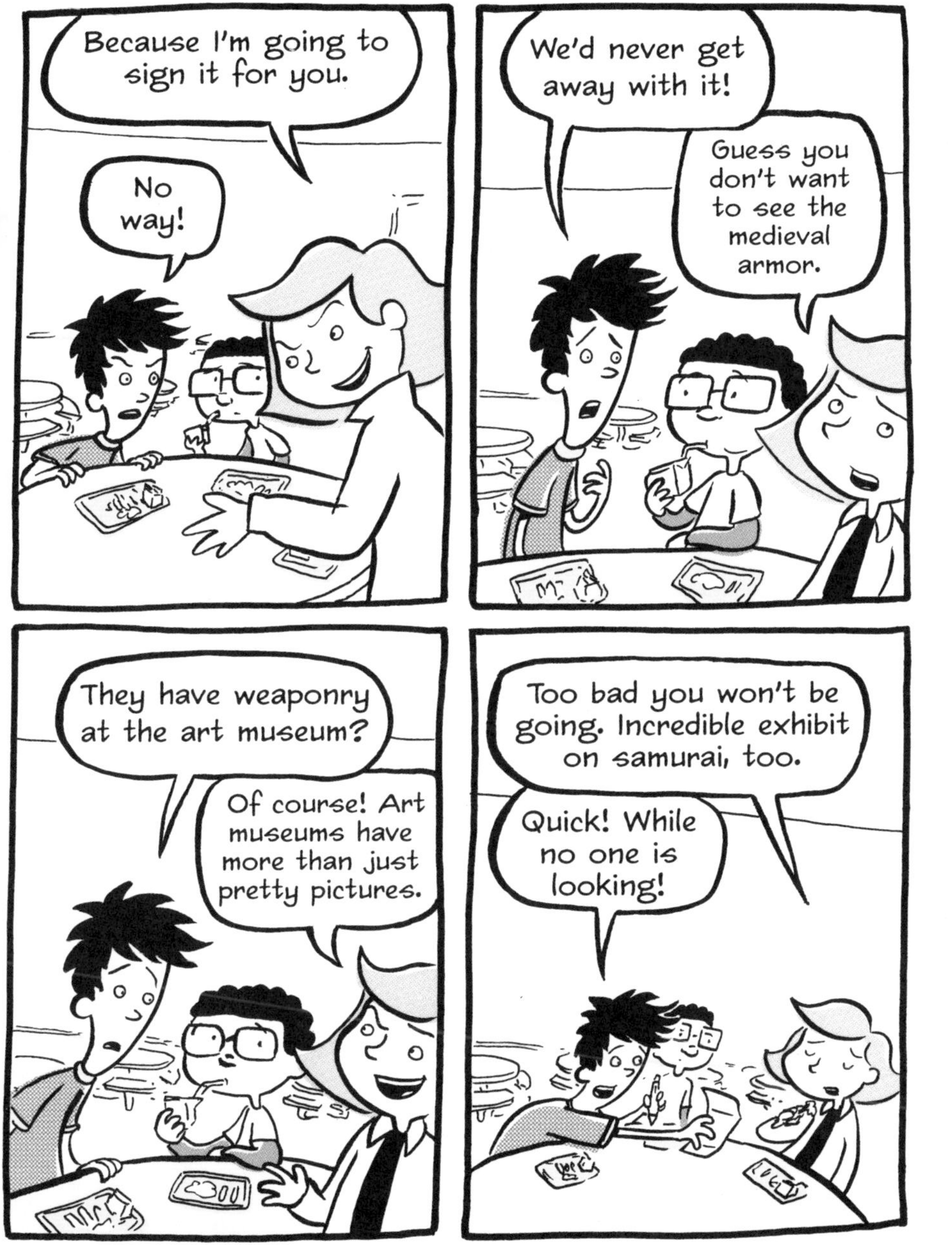
Because I'm going to sign it for you.
No way!
We'd never get away with it!
Guess you don't want to see the medieval armor.
They have weaponry at the art museum?
Of course! Art museums have more than just pretty pictures.
Too bad you won't be going. Incredible exhibit on samurai, too.
Quick! While no one is looking!

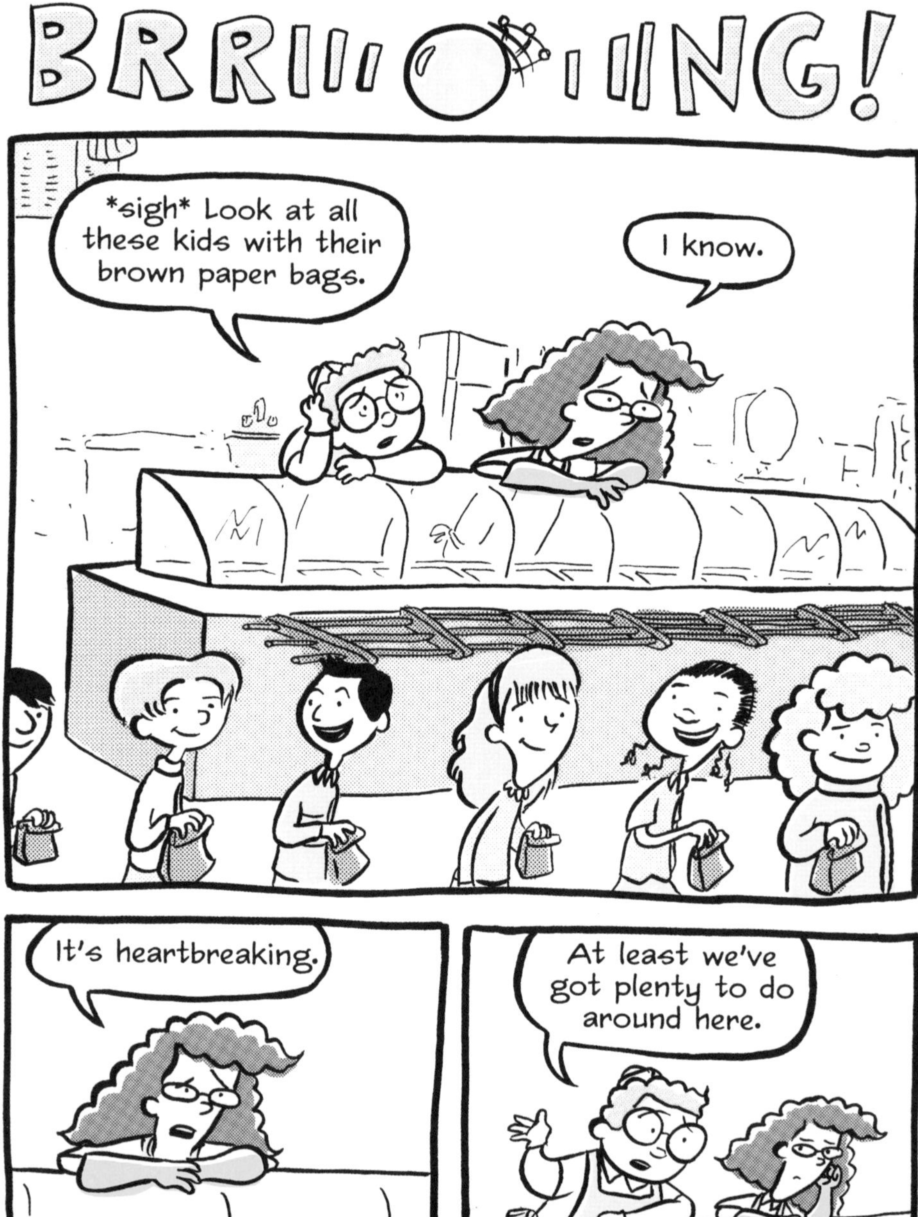
BRRIIIIIIIIING!
sigh Look at all these kids with their brown paper bags.
I know.
It's heartbreaking.
At least we've got plenty to do around here.

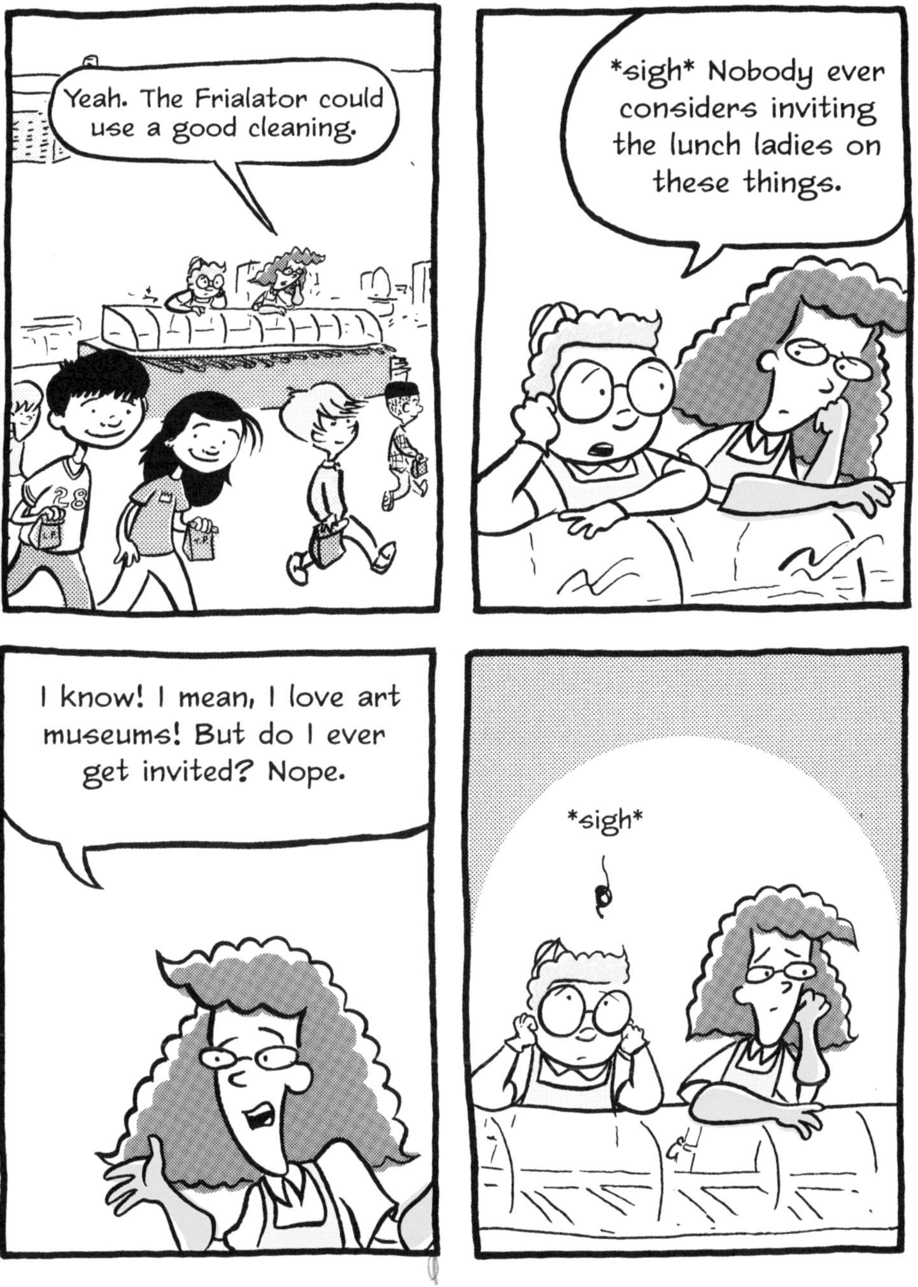
Yeah. The Frialator could use a good cleaning.
sigh Nobody ever considers inviting the lunch ladies on these things.
I know! I mean, I love art museums! But do I ever get invited? Nope.
sigh

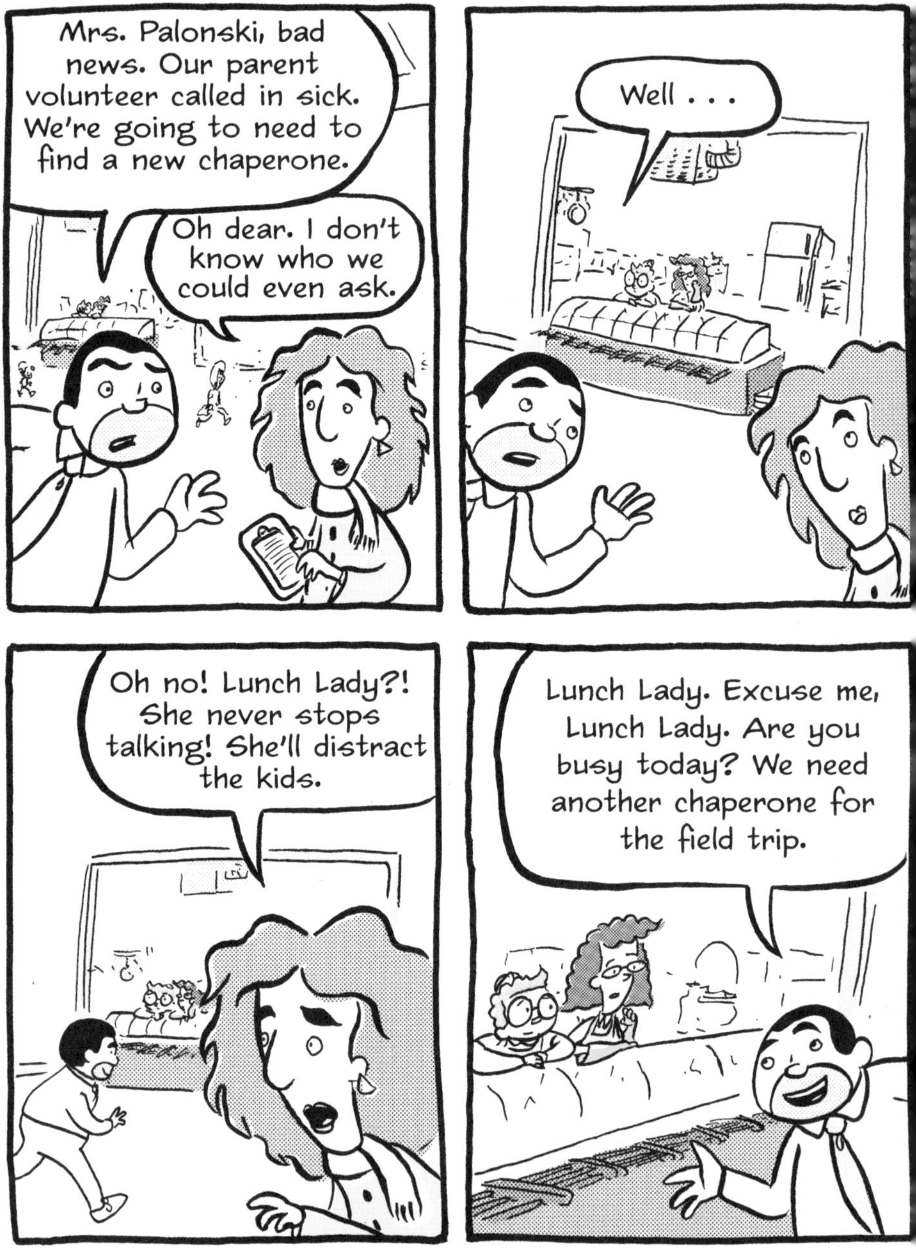
Mrs. Palonski, bad news. Our parent volunteer called in sick. We're going to need to find a new chaperone.
Oh dear. I don't know who we could even ask.
Well . . .
Oh no! Lunch Lady?! She never stops talking! She'll distract the kids.
Lunch Lady. Excuse me, Lunch Lady. Are you busy today? We need another chaperone for the field trip.

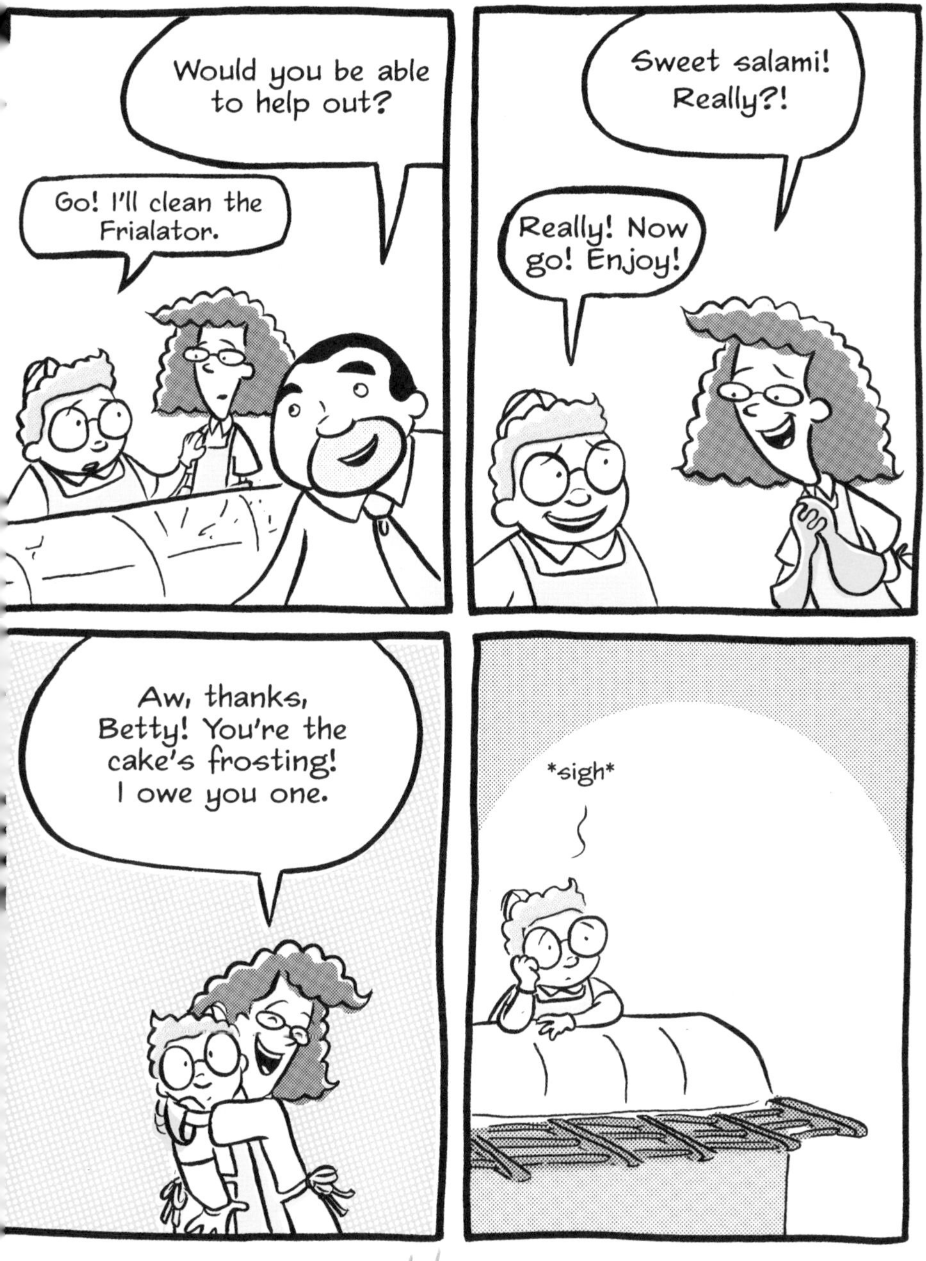
Would you be able to help out?
Go! I'll clean the Frialator.
Sweet salami! Really?!
Really! Now go! Enjoy!
Aw, thanks, Betty! You're the cake's frosting! I owe you one.
sigh

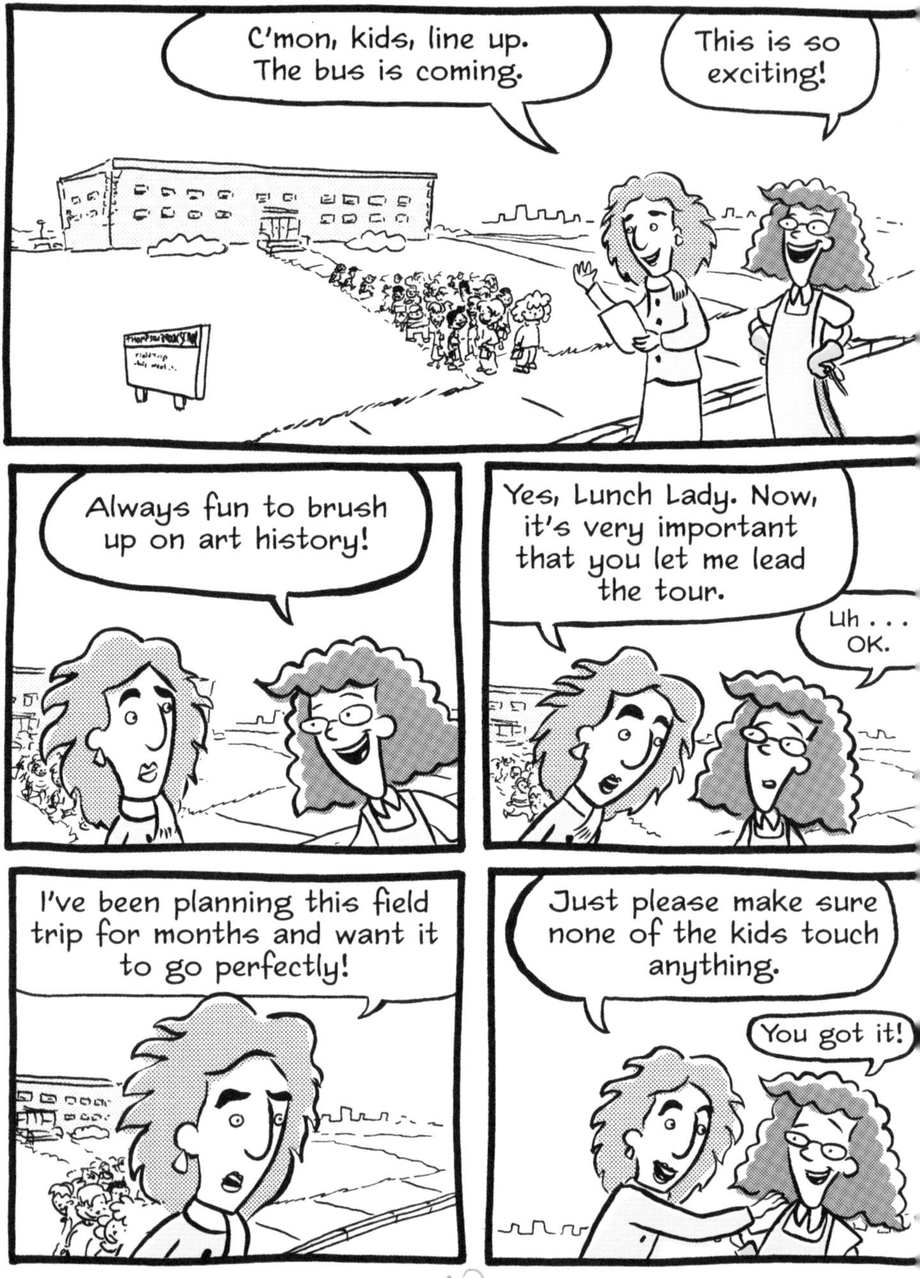
C'mon, kids, line up. The bus is coming.
This is so exciting!
Always fun to brush up on art history!
Yes, Lunch Lady. Now, it's very important that you let me lead the tour.
Uh . . . OK.
I've been planning this field trip for months and want it to go perfectly!
Just please make sure none of the kids touch anything.
You got it!

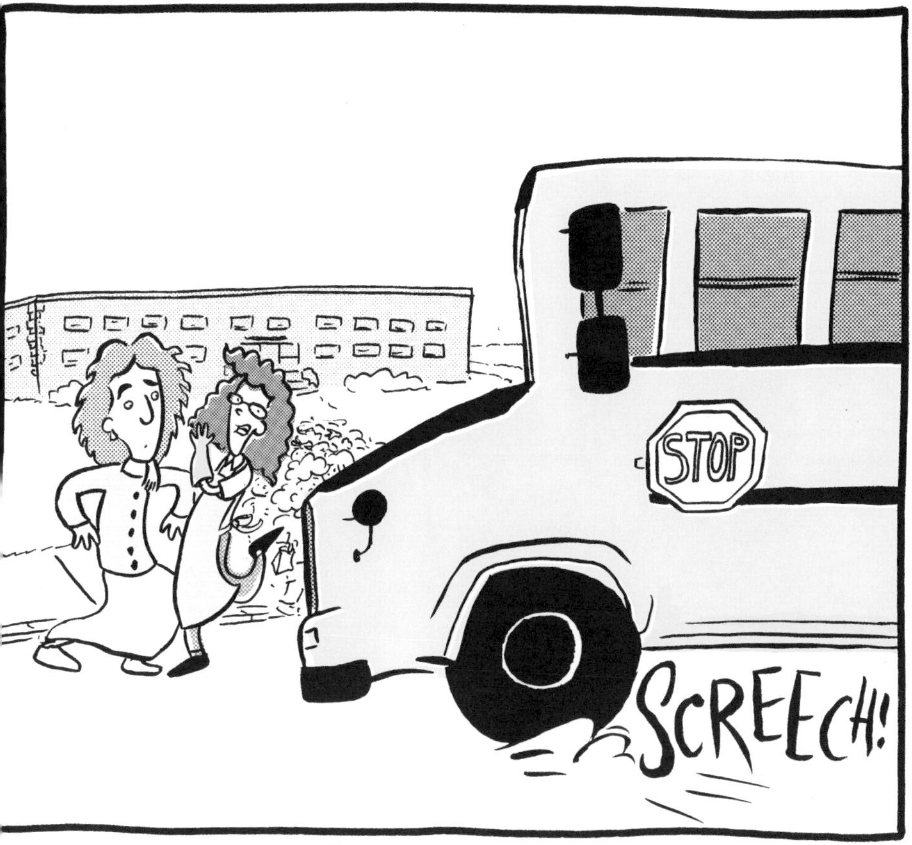
STOP
SCREECH!

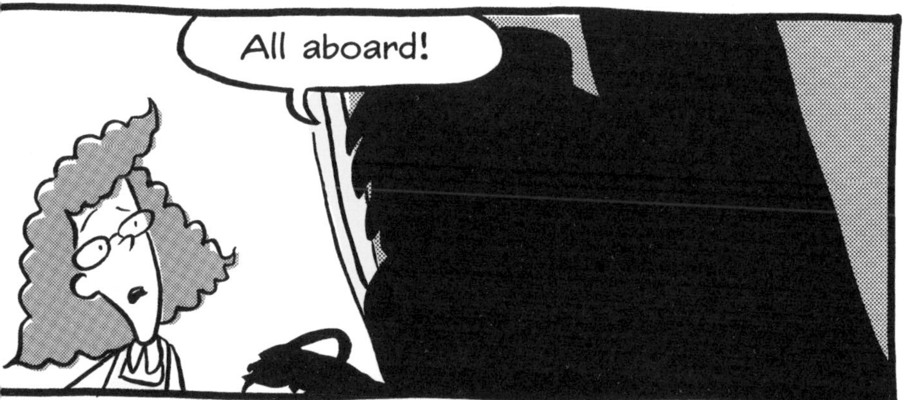
All aboard!

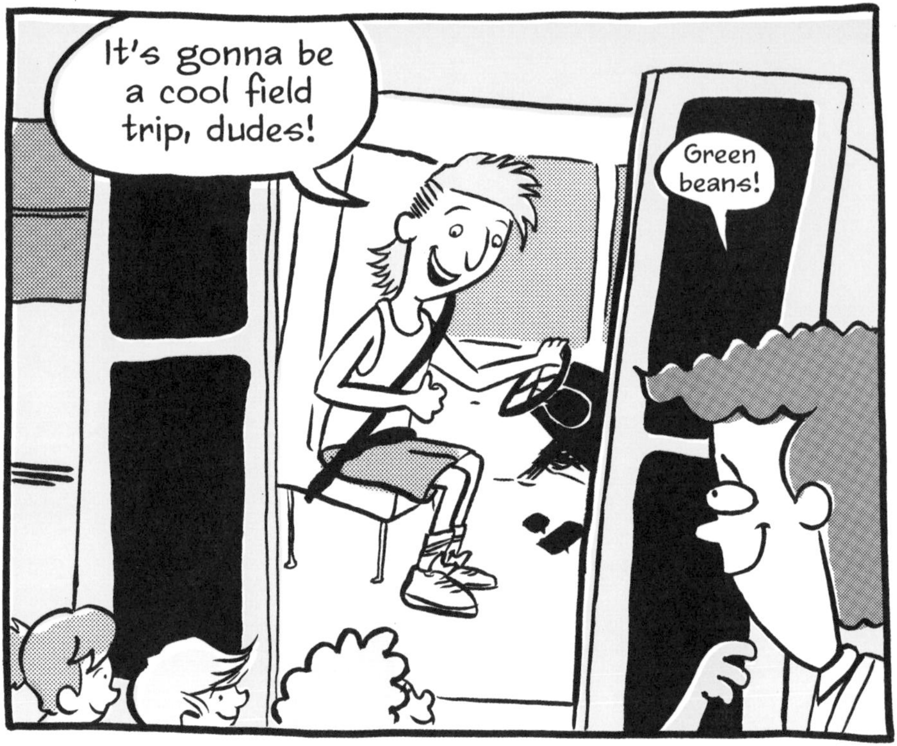
It's gonna be a cool field trip, dudes!
Green beans!

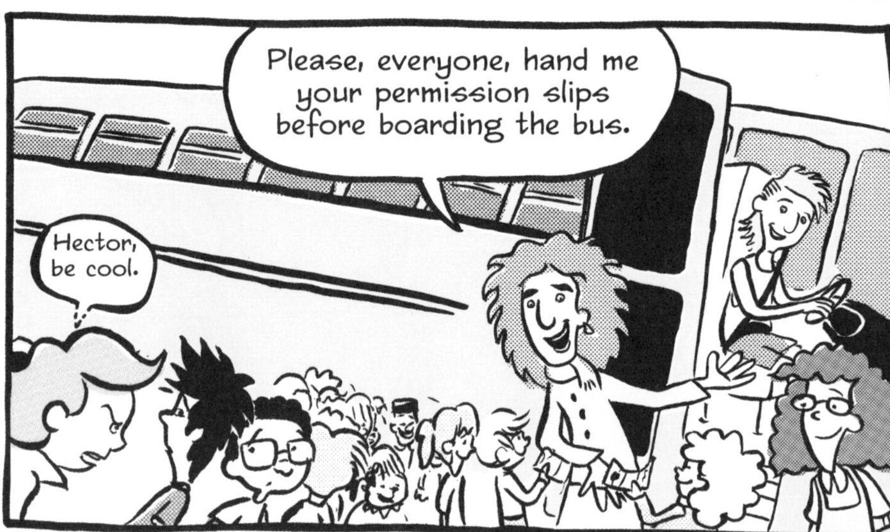
Please, everyone, hand me your permission slips before boarding the bus.
Hector, be cool.

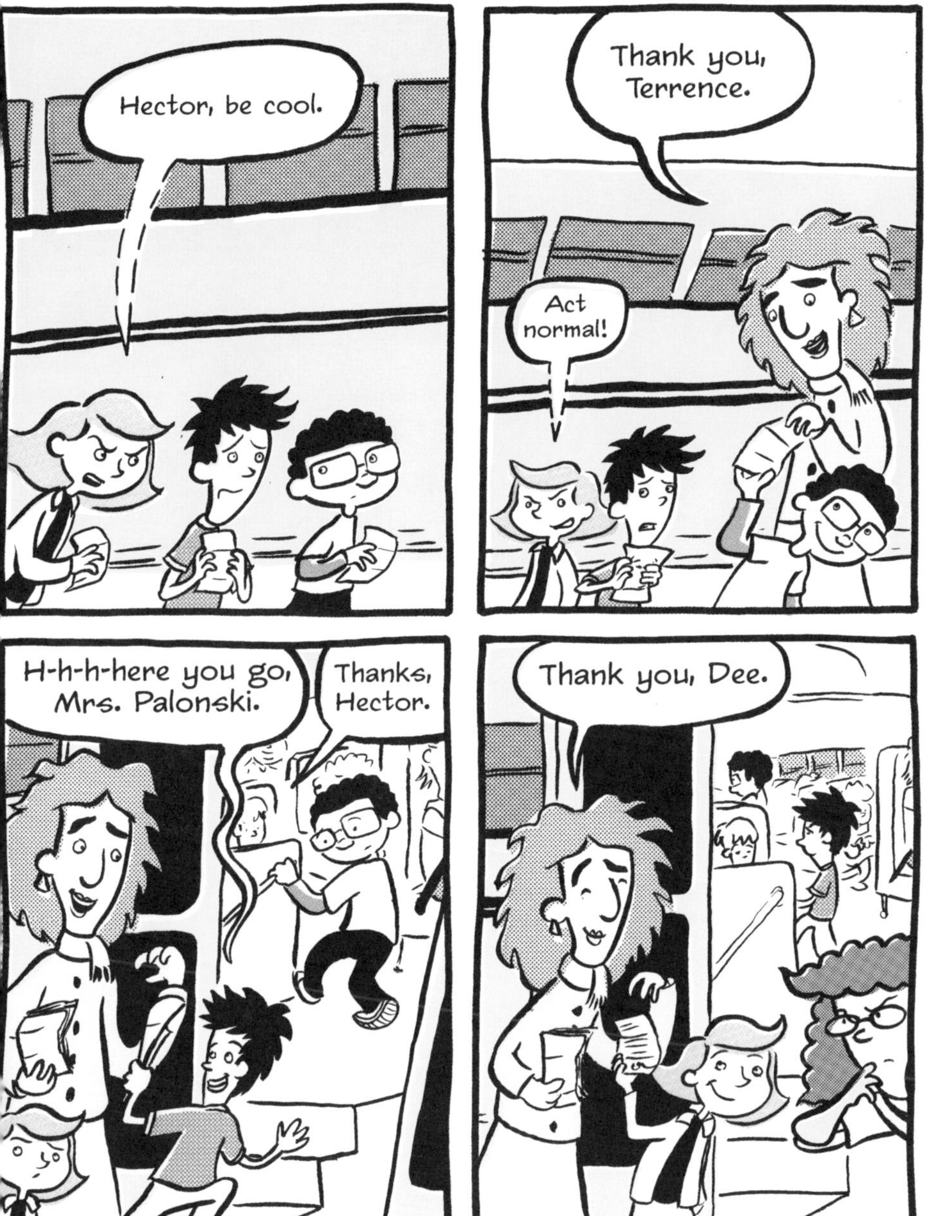
Hector, be cool.
Thank you, Terrence.
Act normal!
H-h-h-here you go, Mrs. Palonski.
Thanks, Hector.
Thank you, Dee.

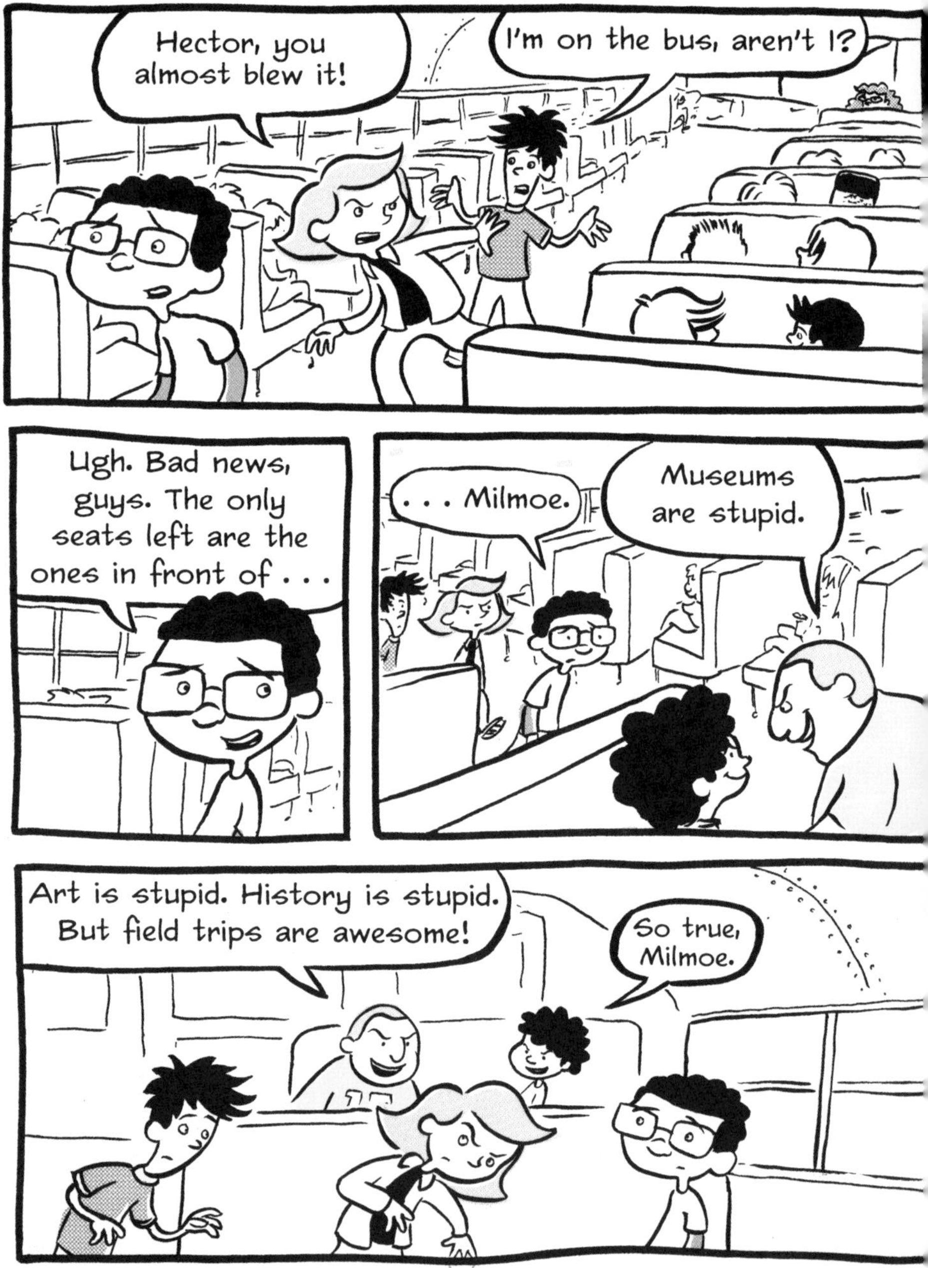
Hector, you almost blew it!
I'm on the bus, aren't I?
Ugh. Bad news, guys. The only seats left are the ones in front of . . .
. . . Milmoe.
Museums are stupid.
Art is stupid. History is stupid. But field trips are awesome!
So true, Milmoe.

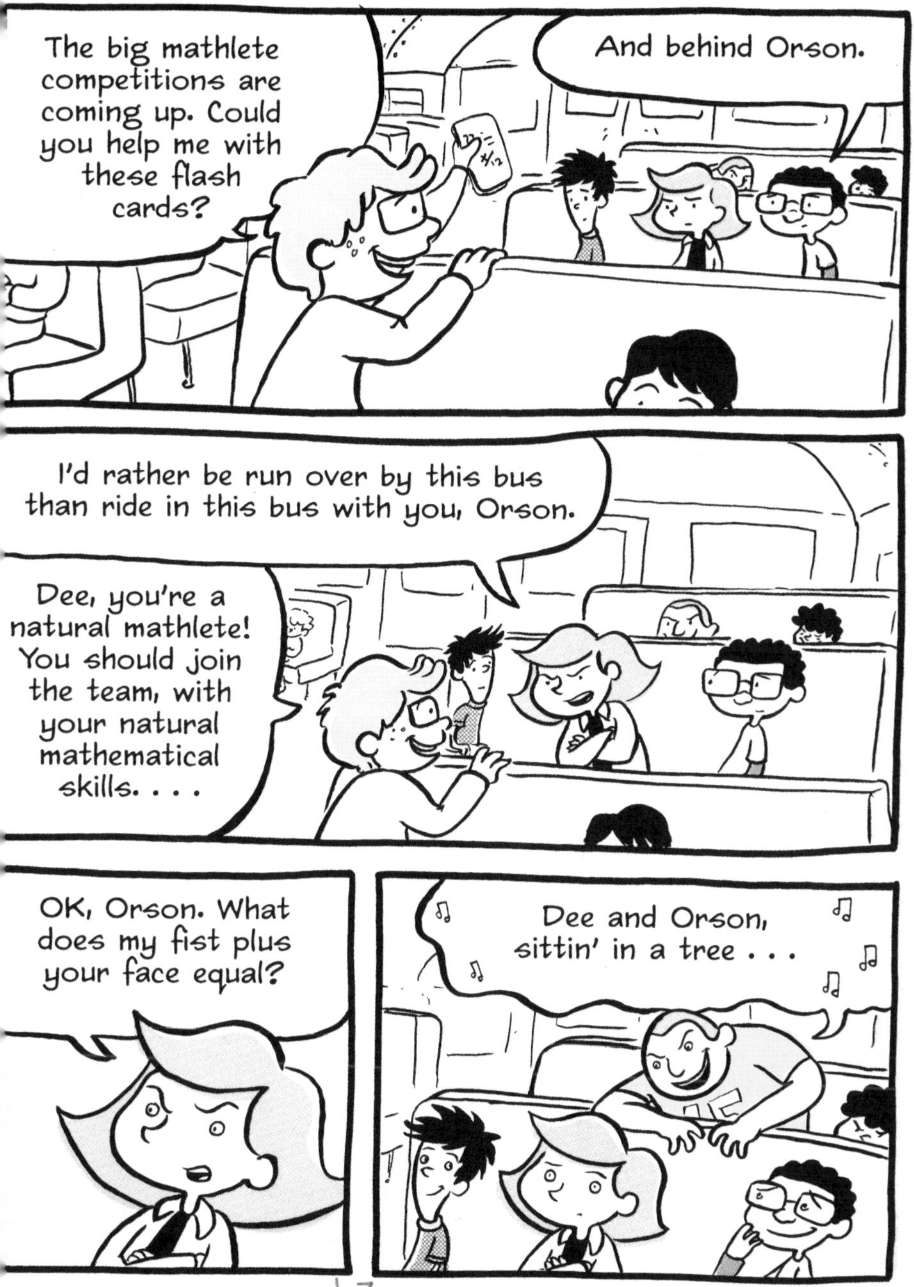
The big mathlete competitions are coming up. Could you help me with these flash cards?
And behind Orson.
I'd rather be run over by this bus than ride in this bus with you, Orson.
Dee, you're a natural mathlete! You should join the team, with your natural mathematical skills. . . .
OK, Orson. What does my fist plus your face equal?
Dee and Orson, sittin' in a tree . . .

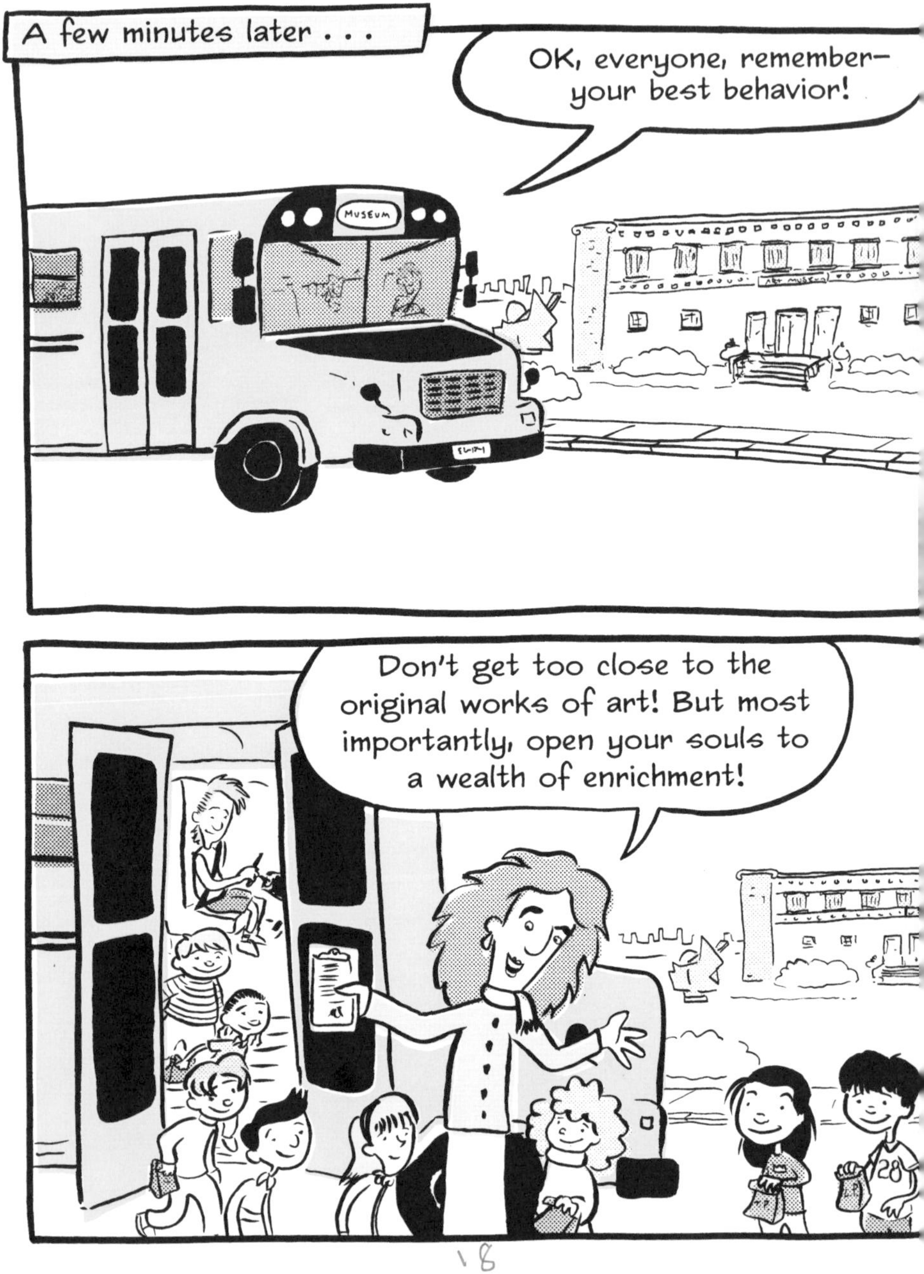
A few minutes later . . .
OK, everyone, remember– your best behavior!
MUSEUM
Don't get too close to the original works of art! But most importantly, open your souls to a wealth of enrichment!
28

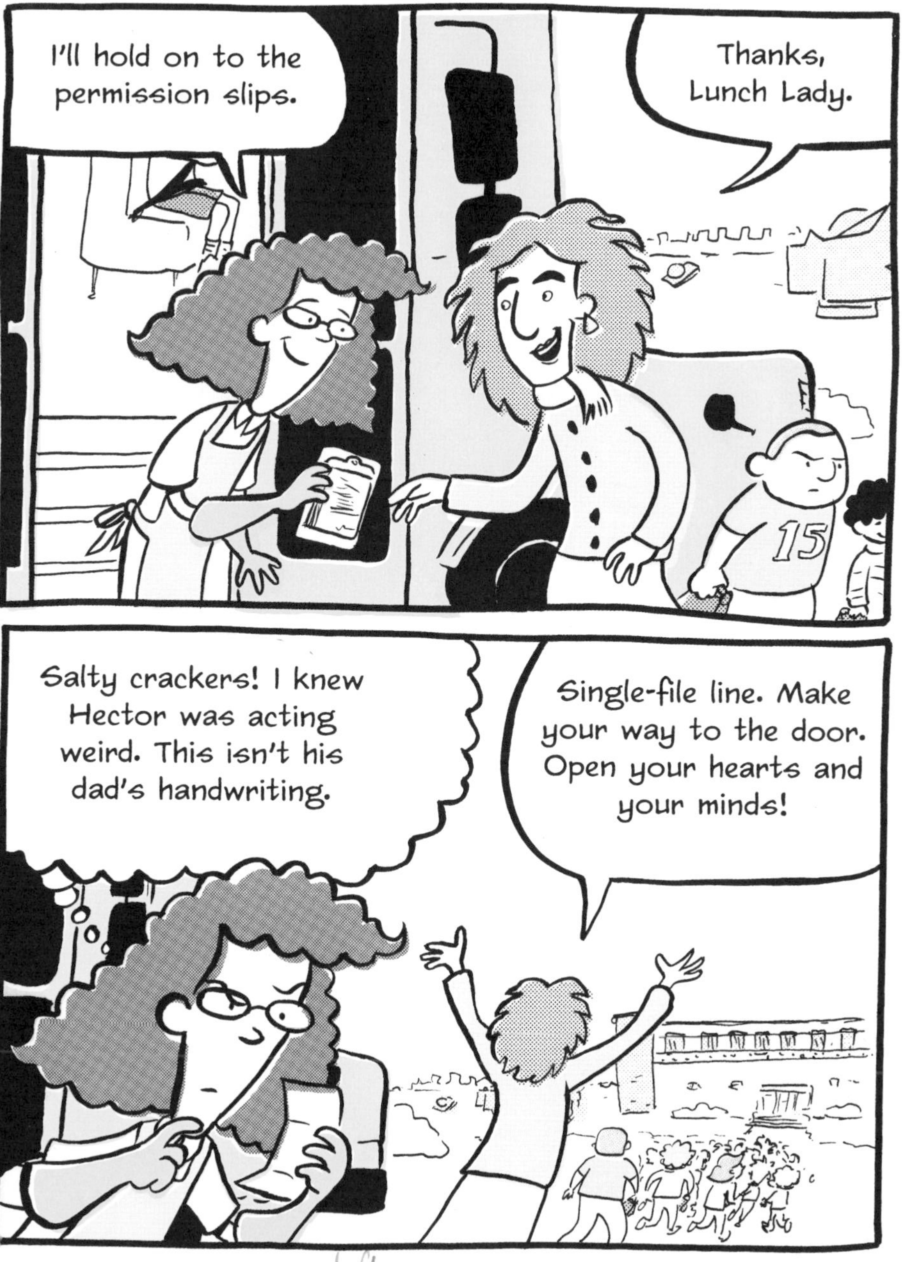
I'll hold on to the permission slips.
Thanks, Lunch Lady.
15
Salty crackers! I knew Hector was acting weird. This isn't his dad's handwriting.
Single-file line. Make your way to the door. Open your hearts and your minds!

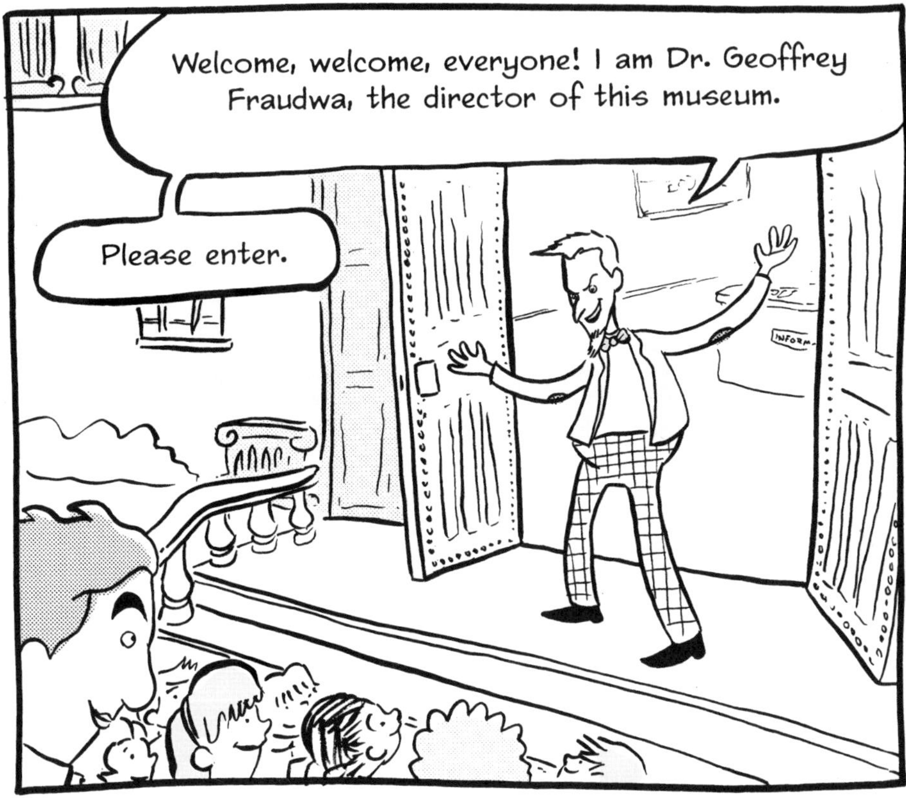
Welcome, welcome, everyone! I am Dr. Geoffrey Fraudwa, the director of this museum.
Please enter.

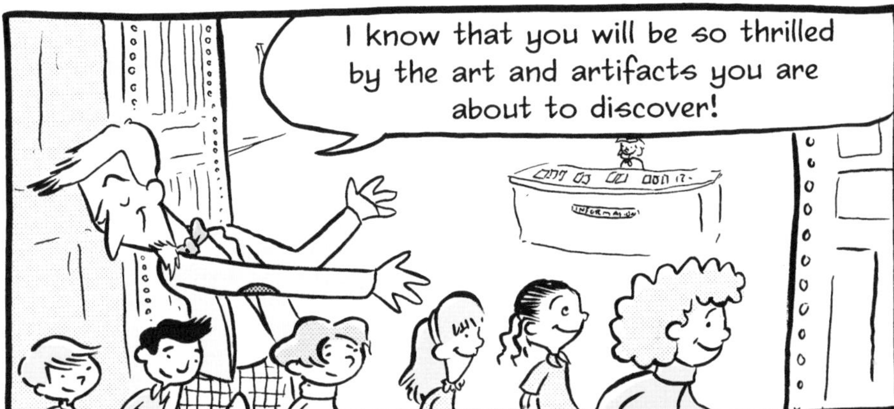
I know that you will be so thrilled by the art and artifacts you are about to discover!

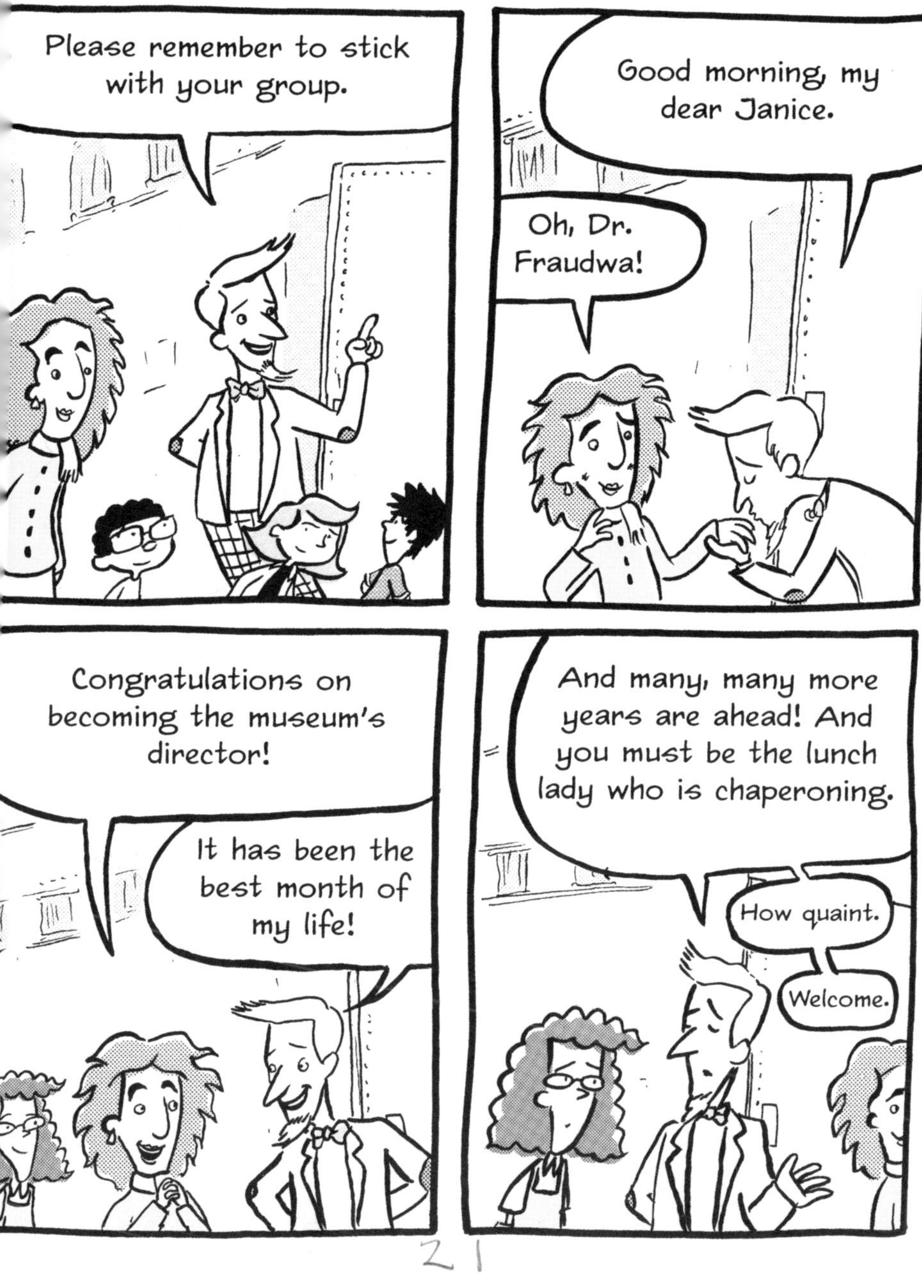
Please remember to stick with your group.
Good morning, my dear Janice.
Oh, Dr. Fraudwa!
Congratulations on becoming the museum's director!
It has been the best month of my life!
And many, many more years are ahead! And you must be the lunch lady who is chaperoning.
How quaint.
Welcome.

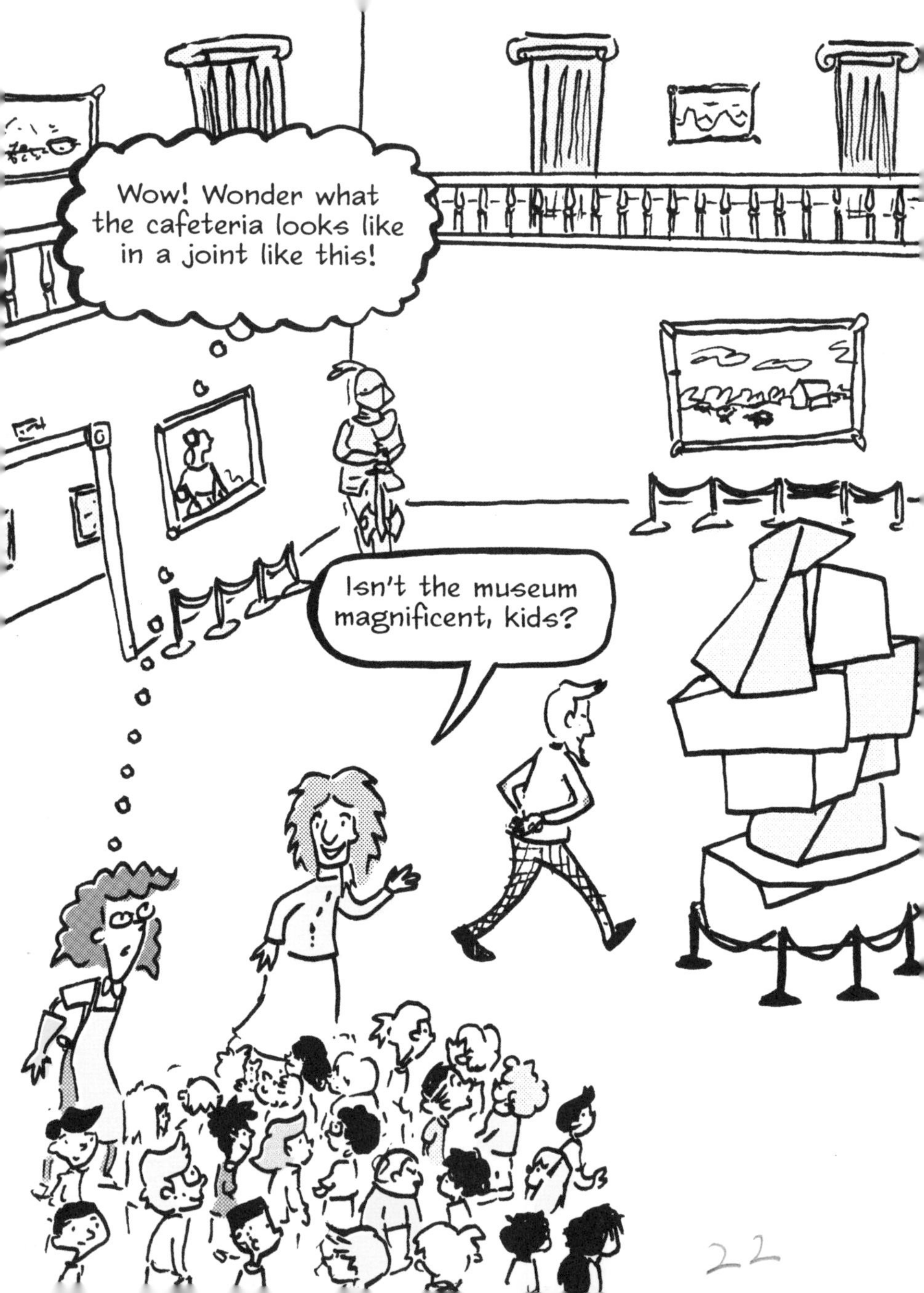
Wow! Wonder what the cafeteria looks like in a joint like this!
Isn't the museum magnificent, kids?

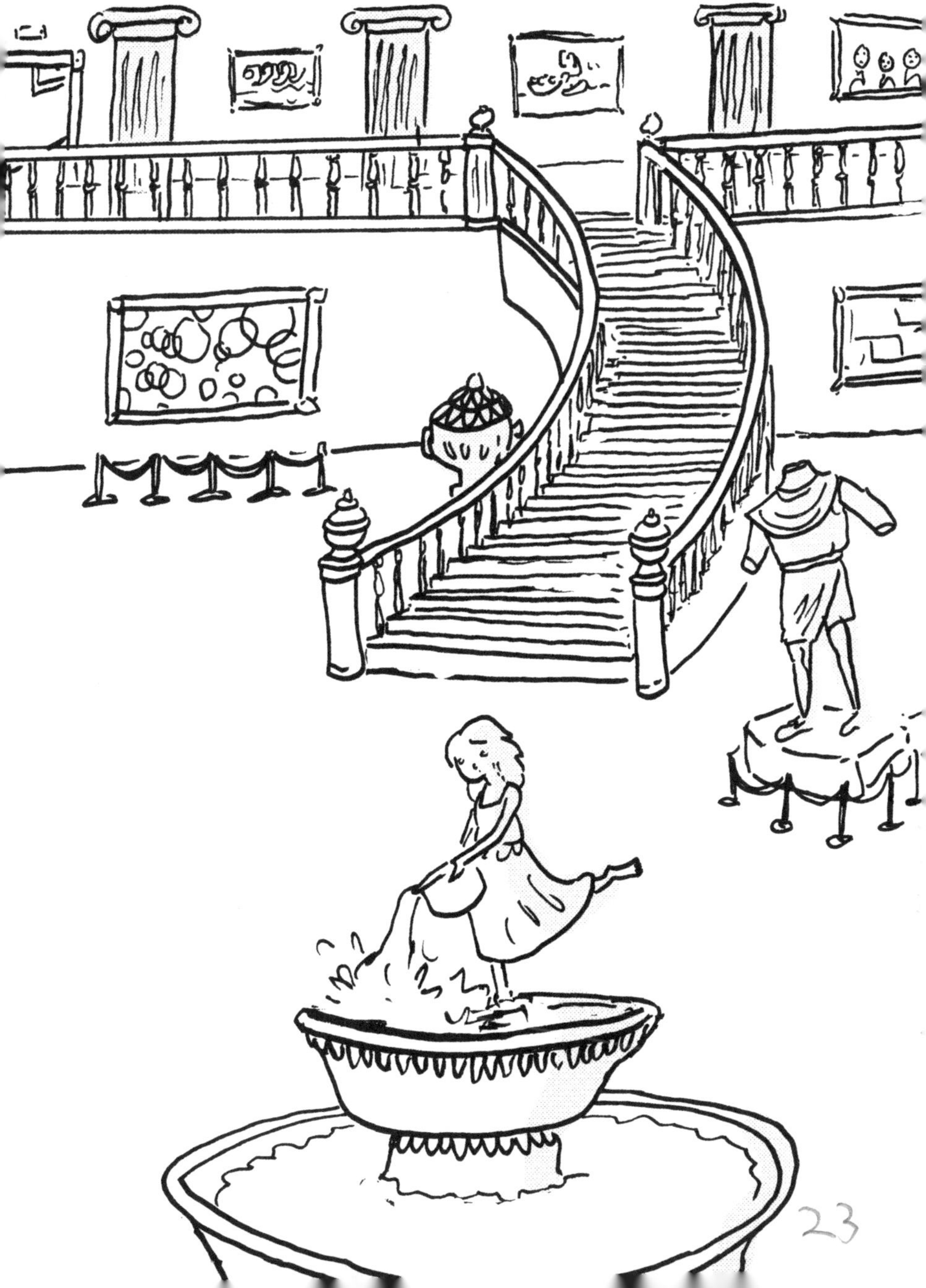

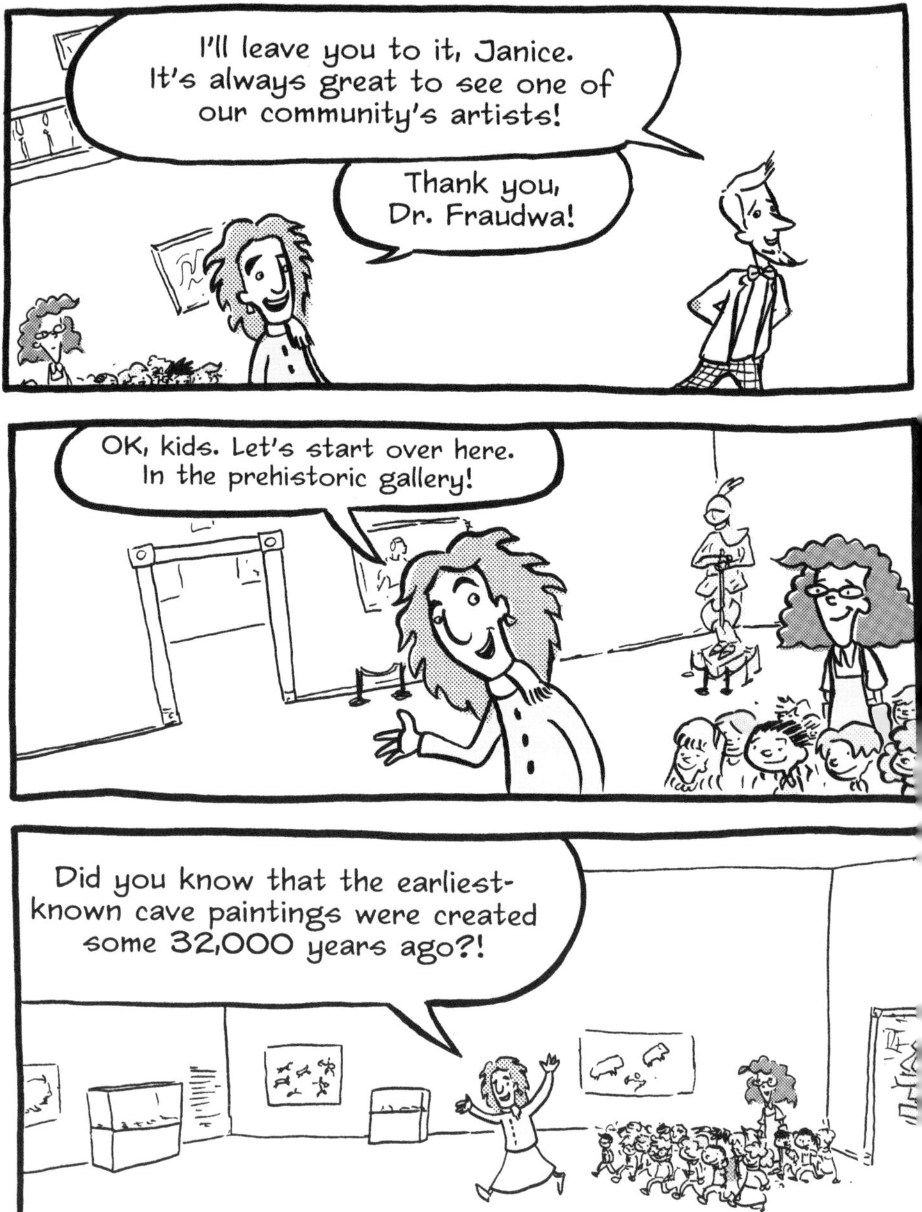
I'll leave you to it, Janice. It's always great to see one of our community's artists!
Thank you, Dr. Fraudwa!
OK, kids. Let's start over here. In the prehistoric gallery!
Did you know that the earliest-known cave paintings were created some 32,000 years ago?!

25

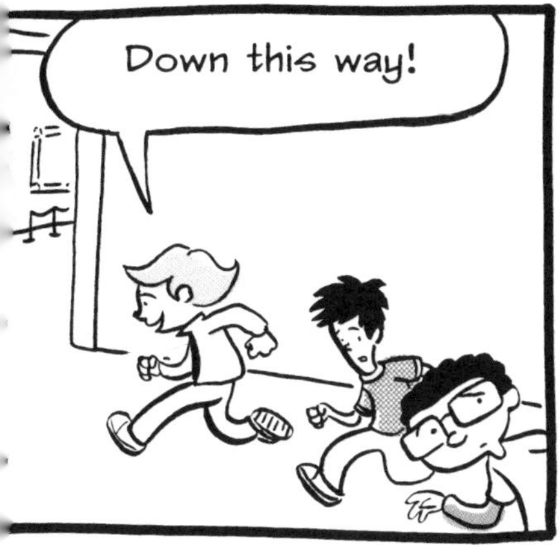
Down this way!

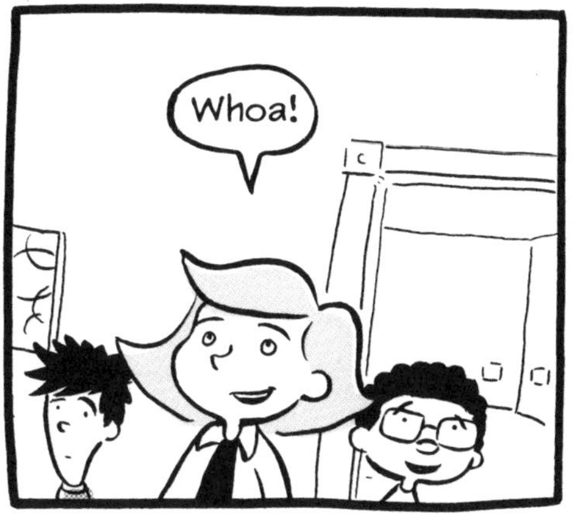
Whoa!

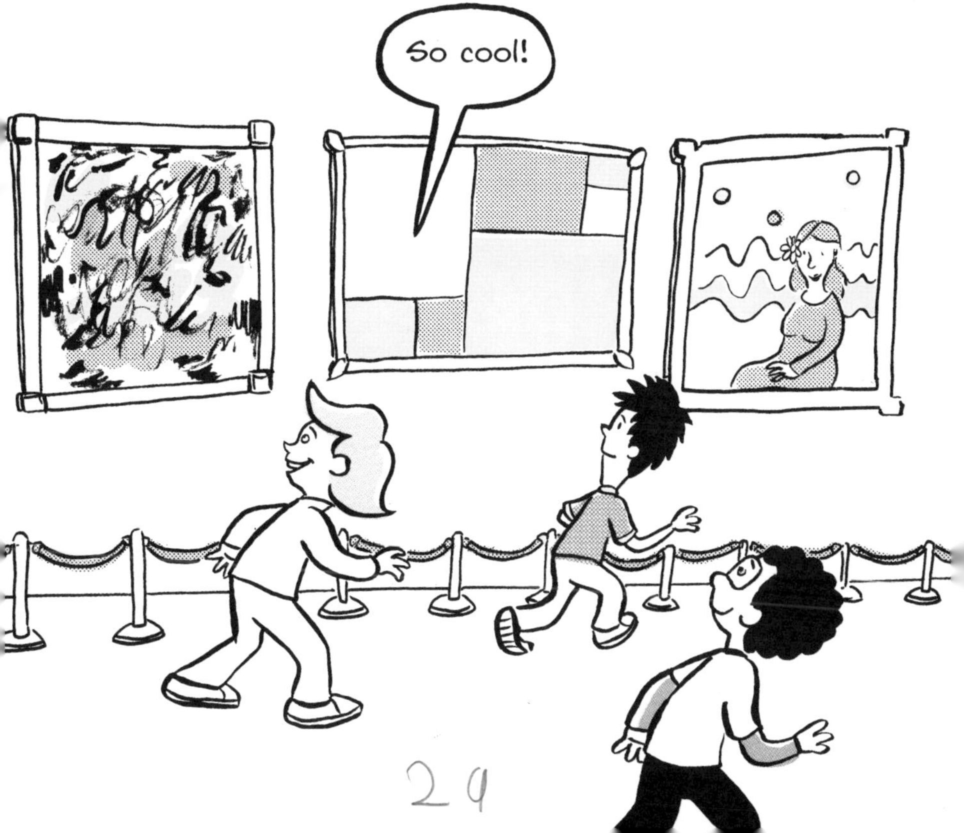
So cool!

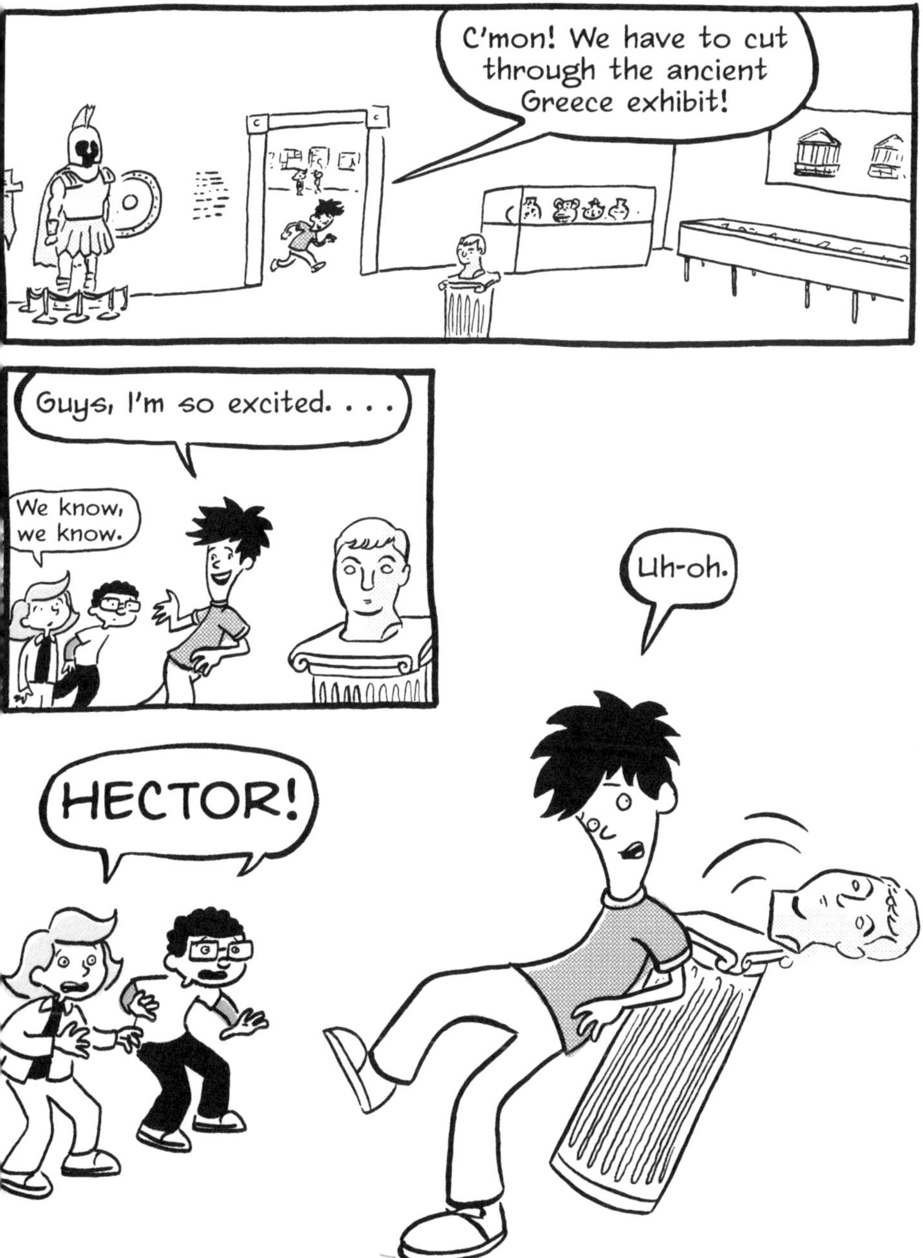
C'mon! We have to cut through the ancient Greece exhibit!
Guys, I'm so excited. . . .
We know, we know.
Uh-oh.
HECTOR!

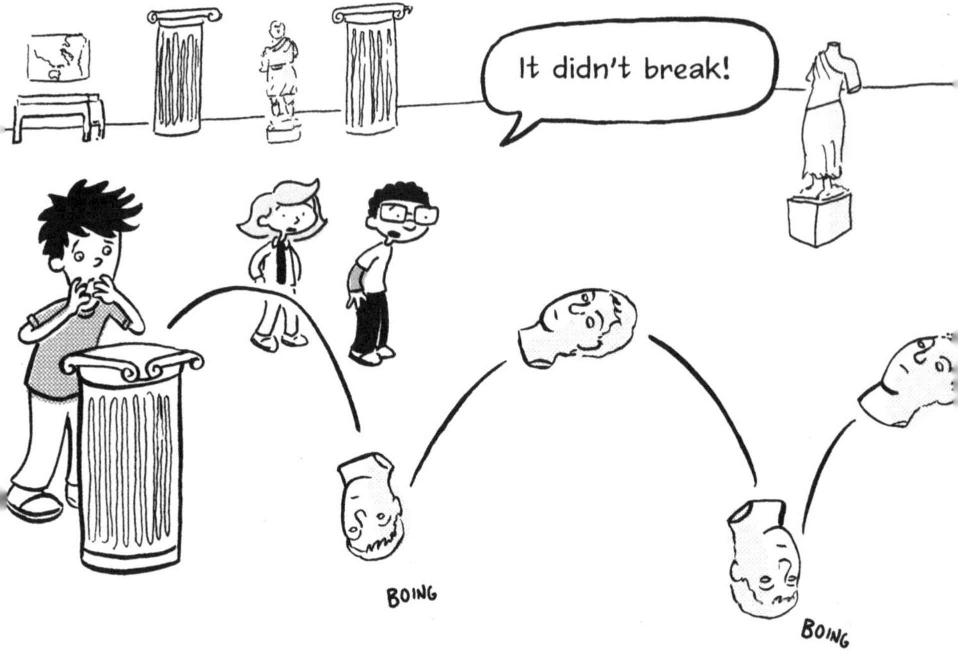
It didn't break!
BOING
BOING

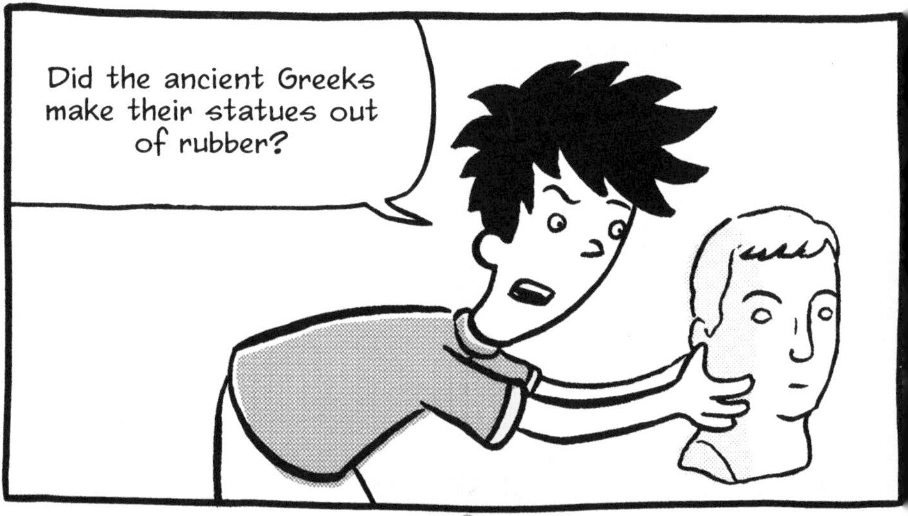
Did the ancient Greeks make their statues out of rubber?

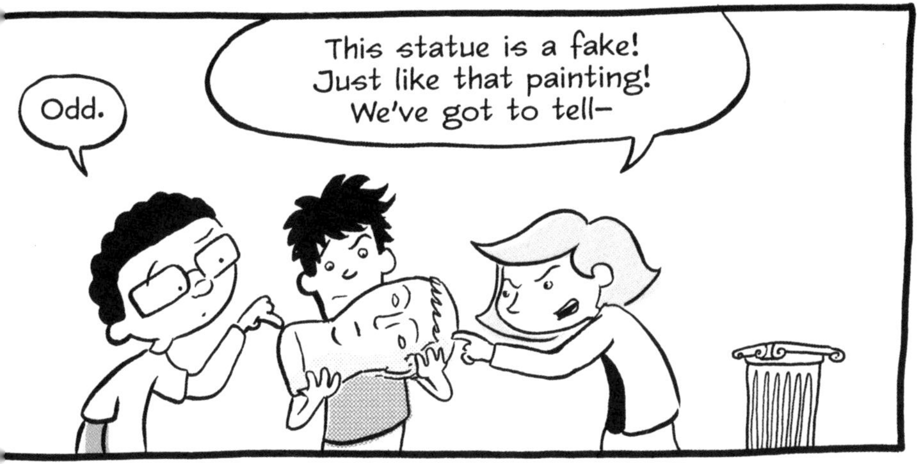
Odd.
This statue is a fake! Just like that painting! We've got to tell–

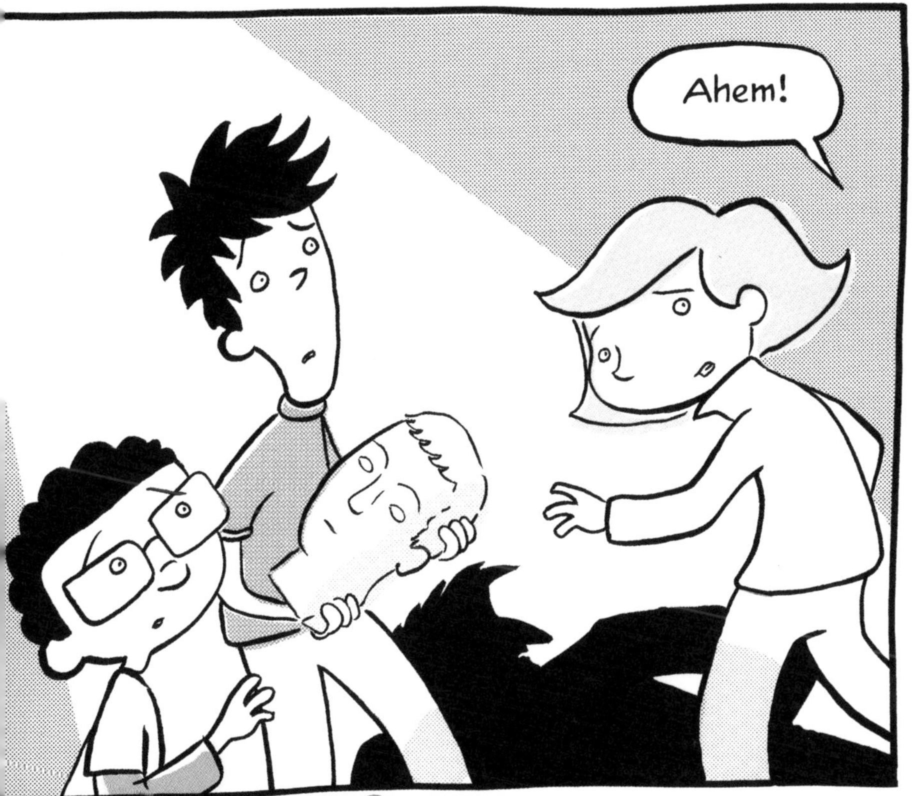
Ahem!

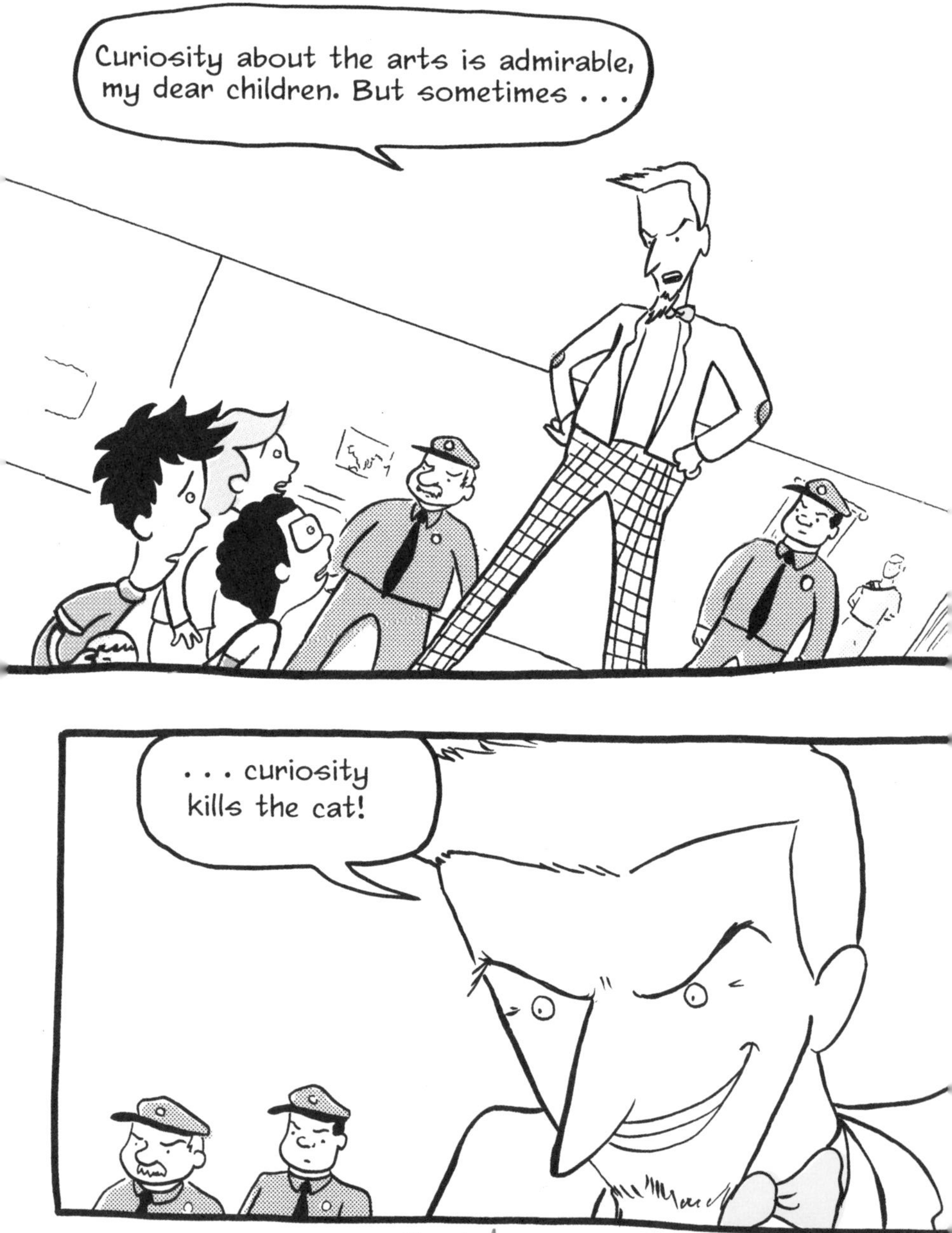
Curiosity about the arts is admirable, my dear children. But sometimes . . .
. . . curiosity kills the cat!

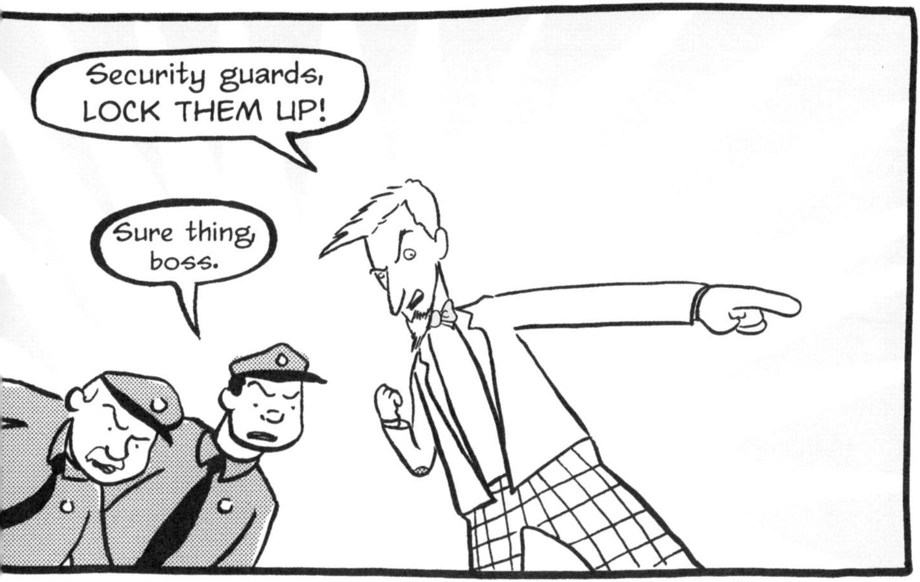
Security guards, LOCK THEM UP!
Sure thing, boss.

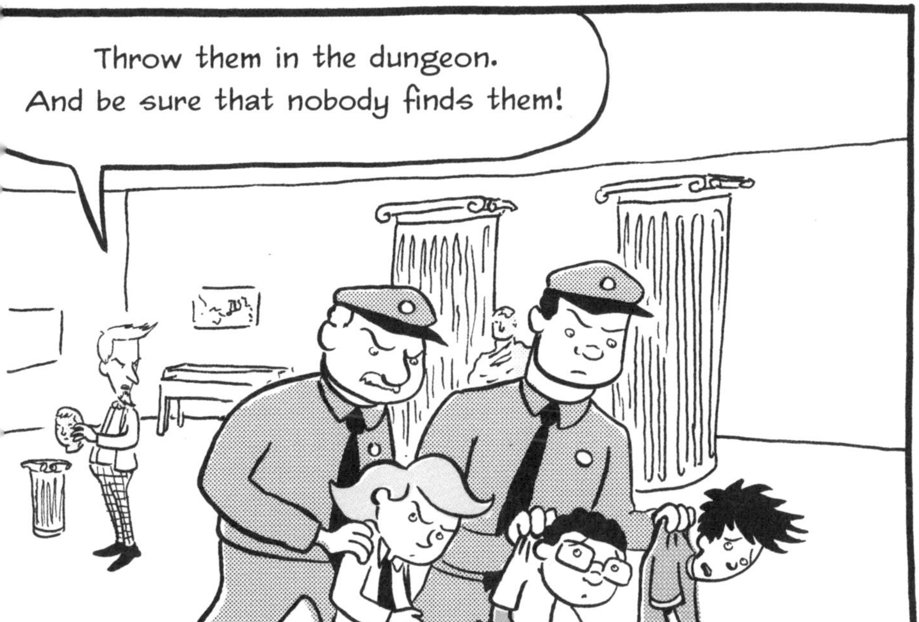
Throw them in the dungeon. And be sure that nobody finds them!

38

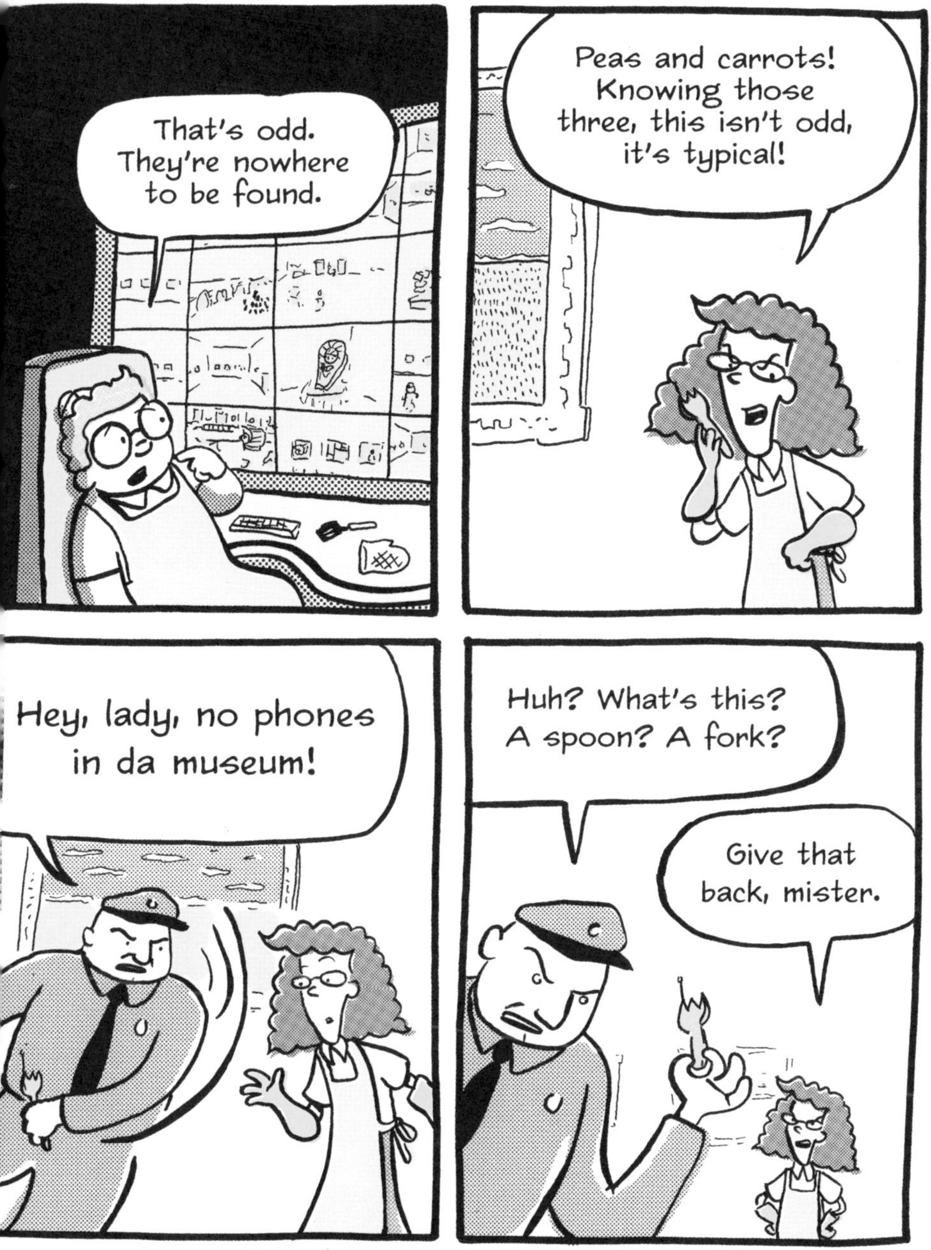
That's odd. They're nowhere to be found.
Peas and carrots! Knowing those three, this isn't odd, it's typical!
Hey, lady, no phones in da museum!
Huh? What's this? A spoon? A fork?
Give that back, mister.

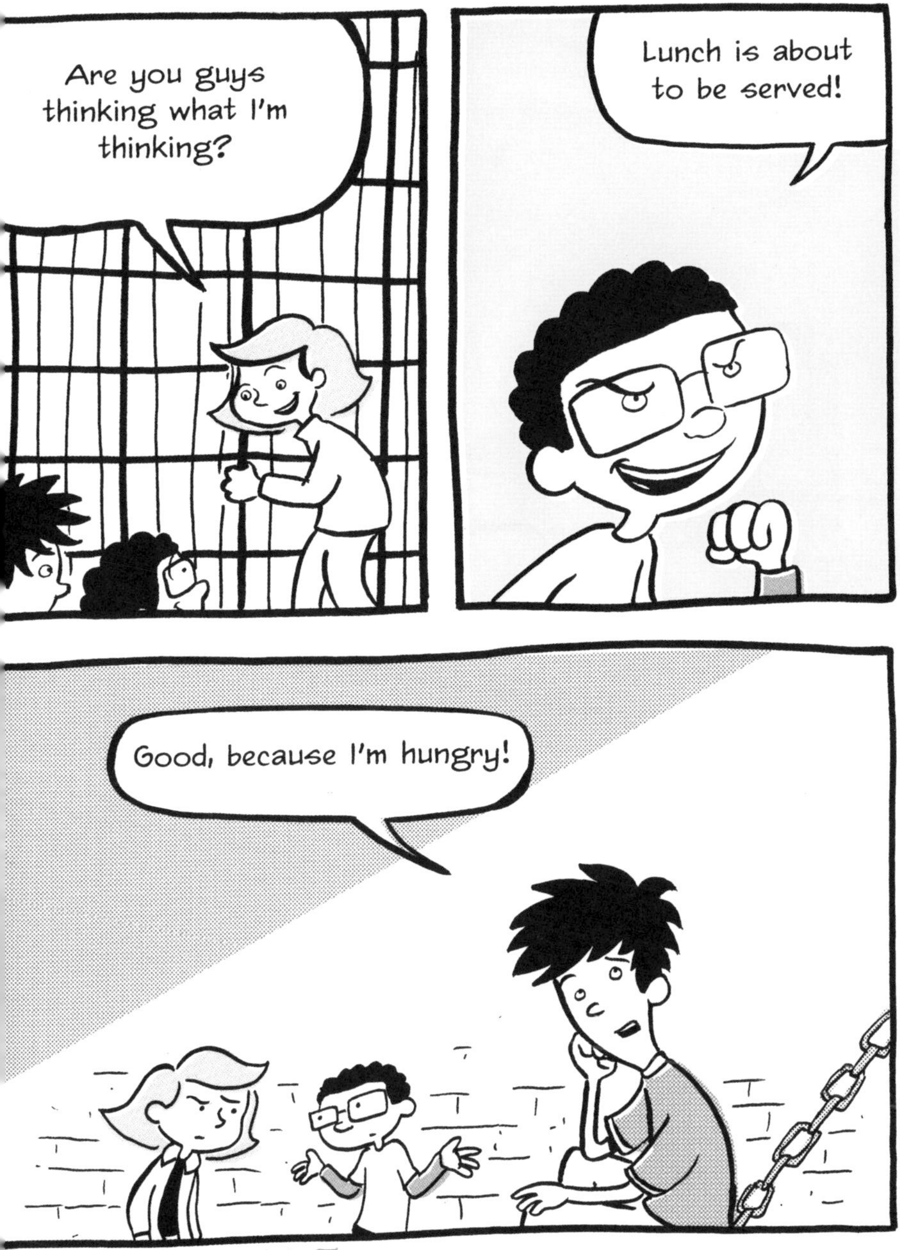
Are you guys thinking what I'm thinking?
Lunch is about to be served!
Good, because I'm hungry!

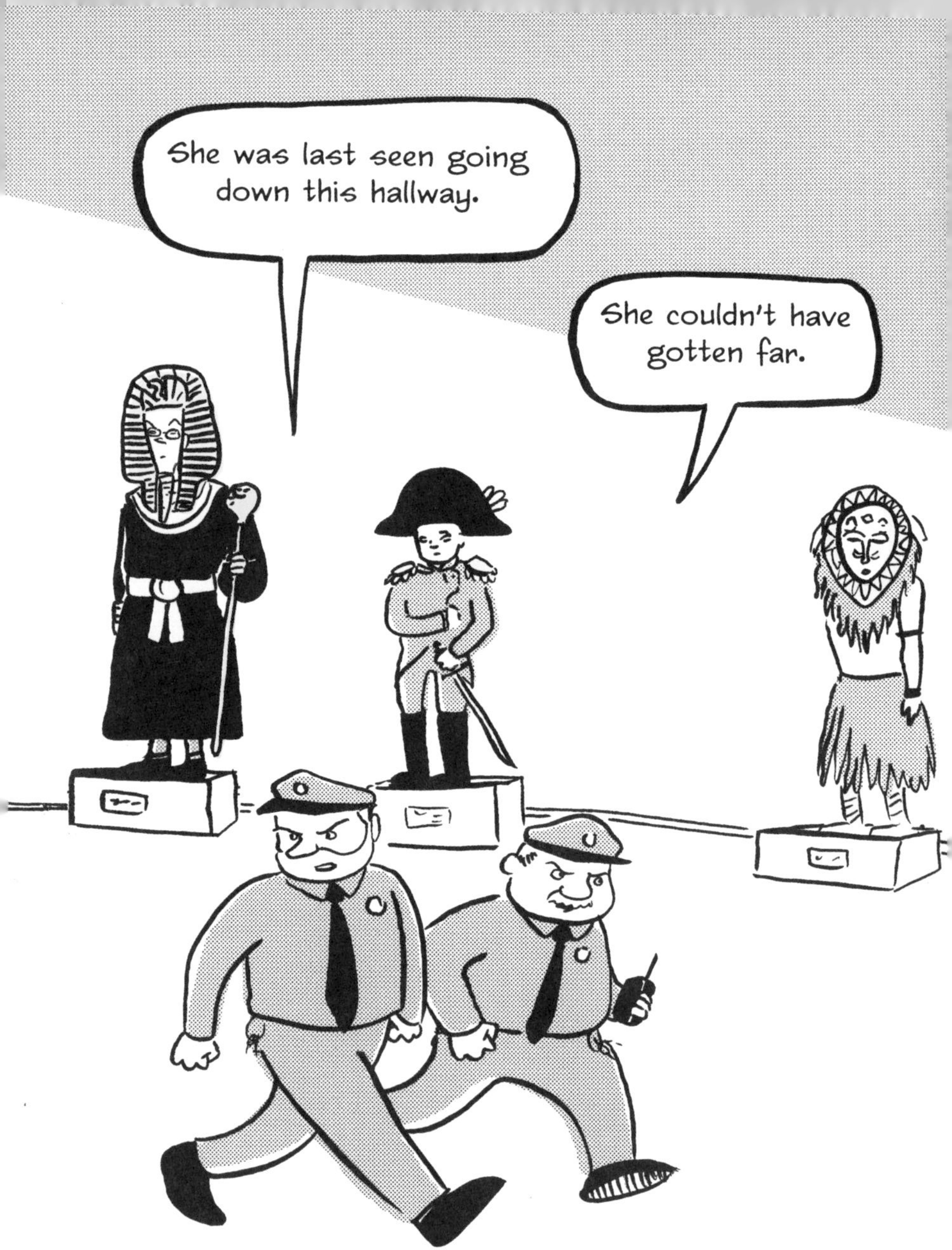
She was last seen going down this hallway.
She couldn't have gotten far.

48

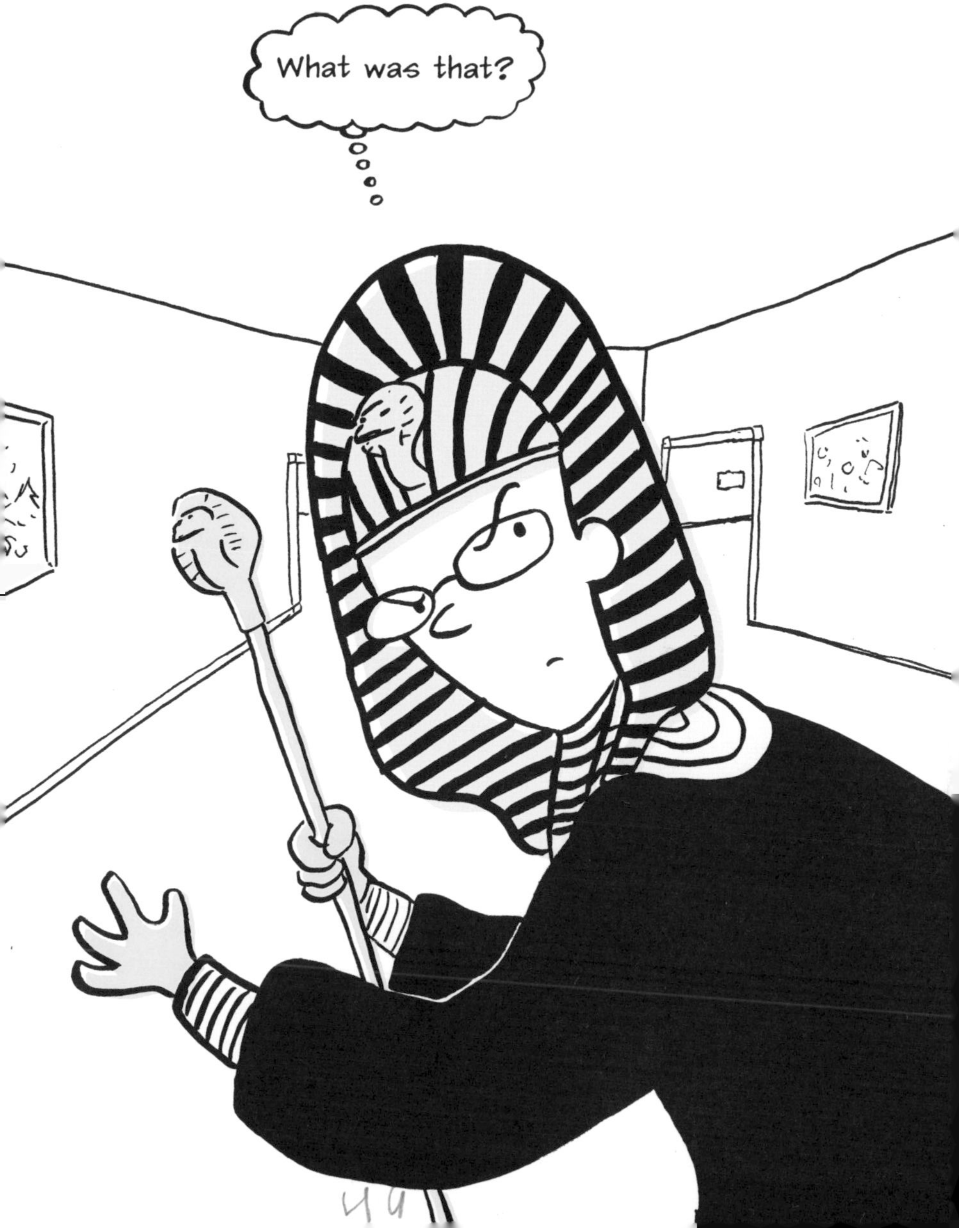
What was that?

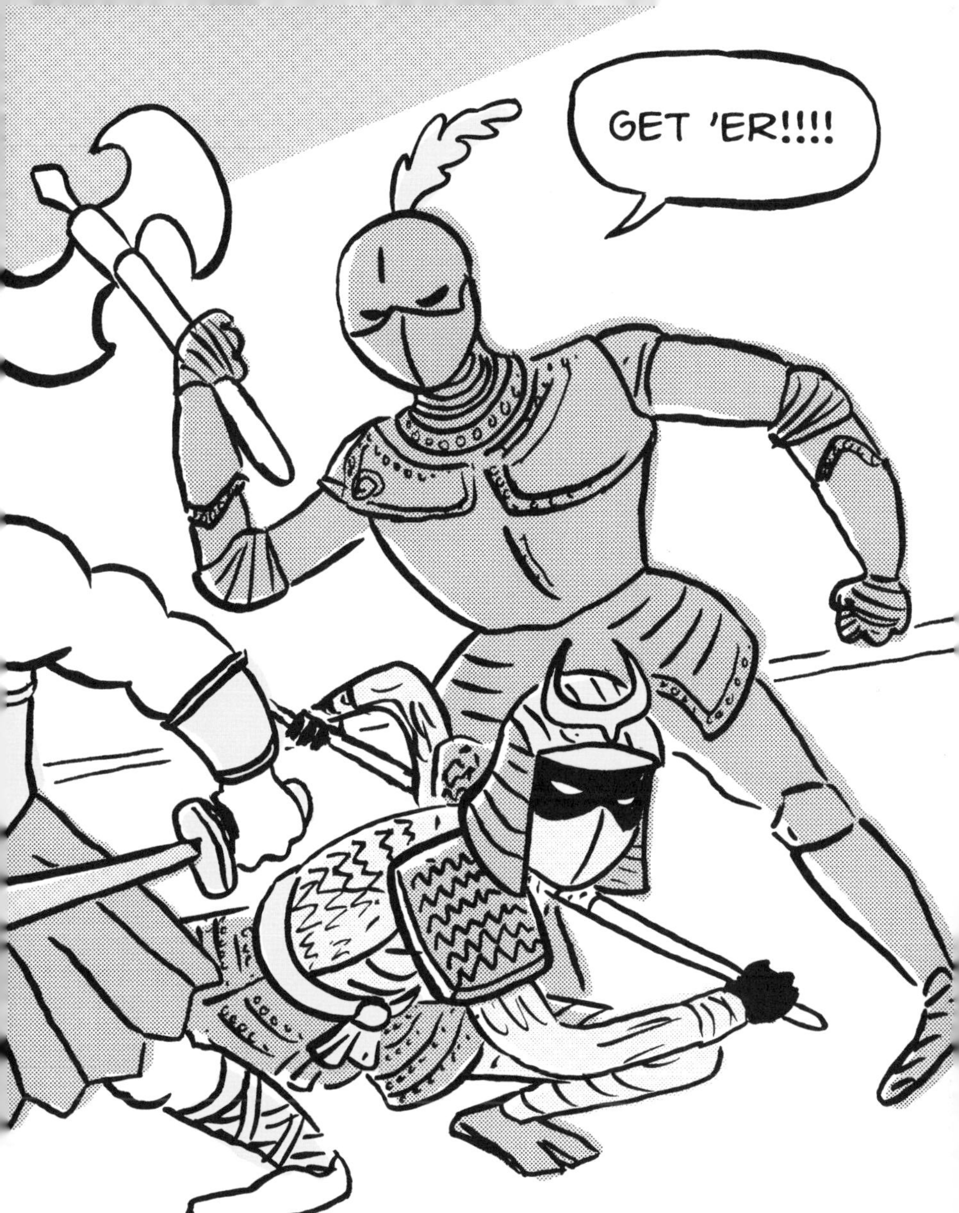
GET 'ER!!!!

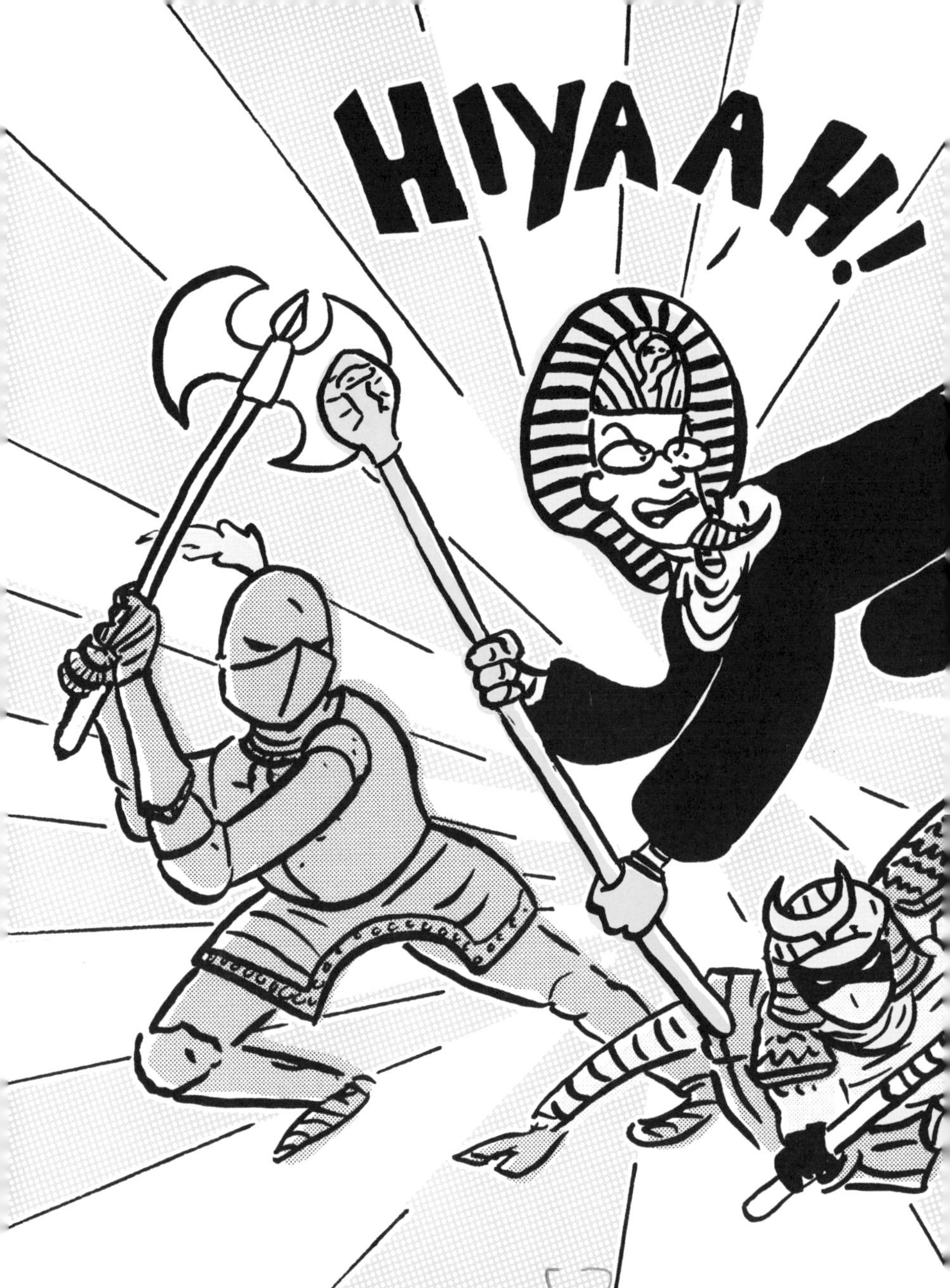
HIYAAH!

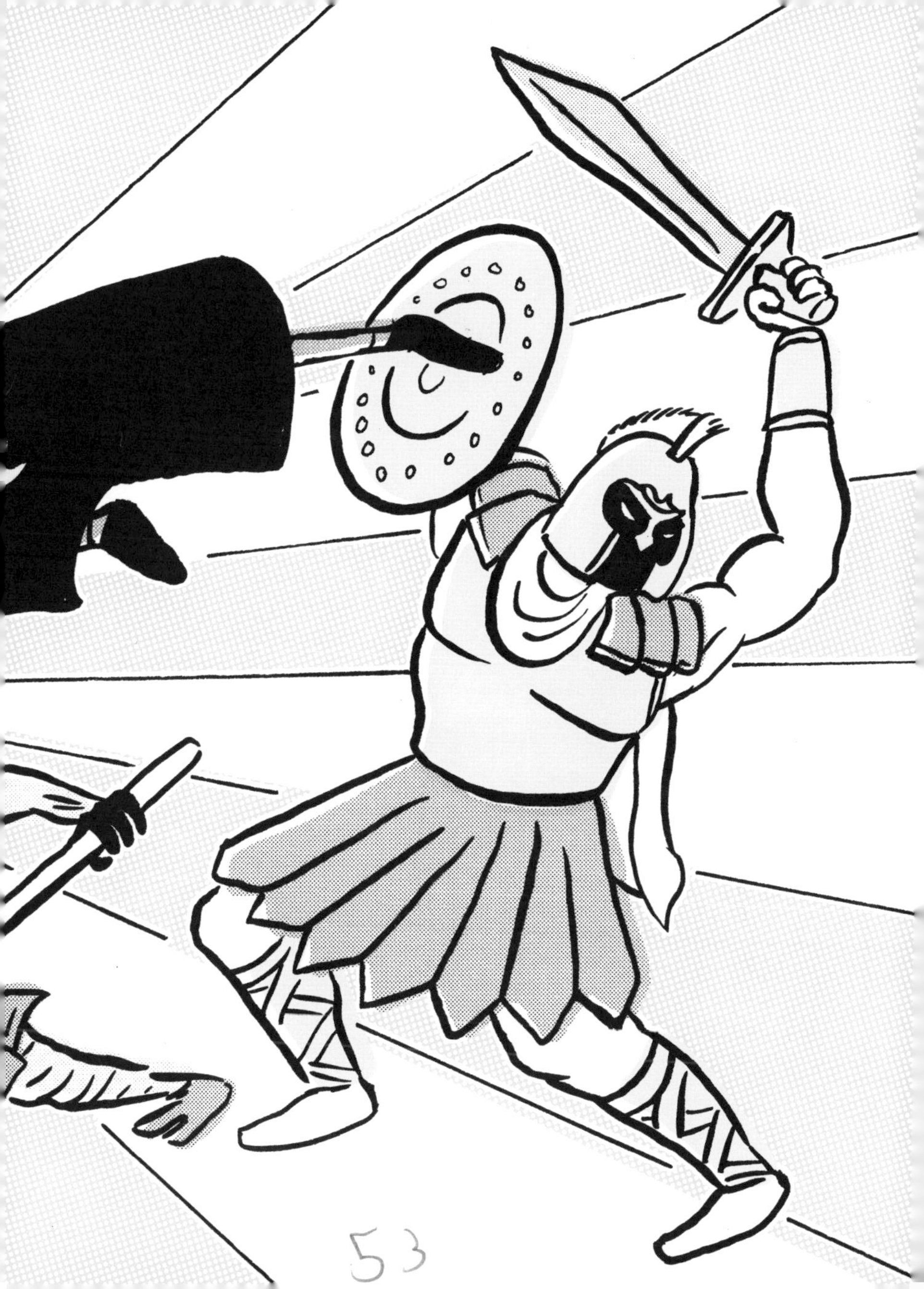

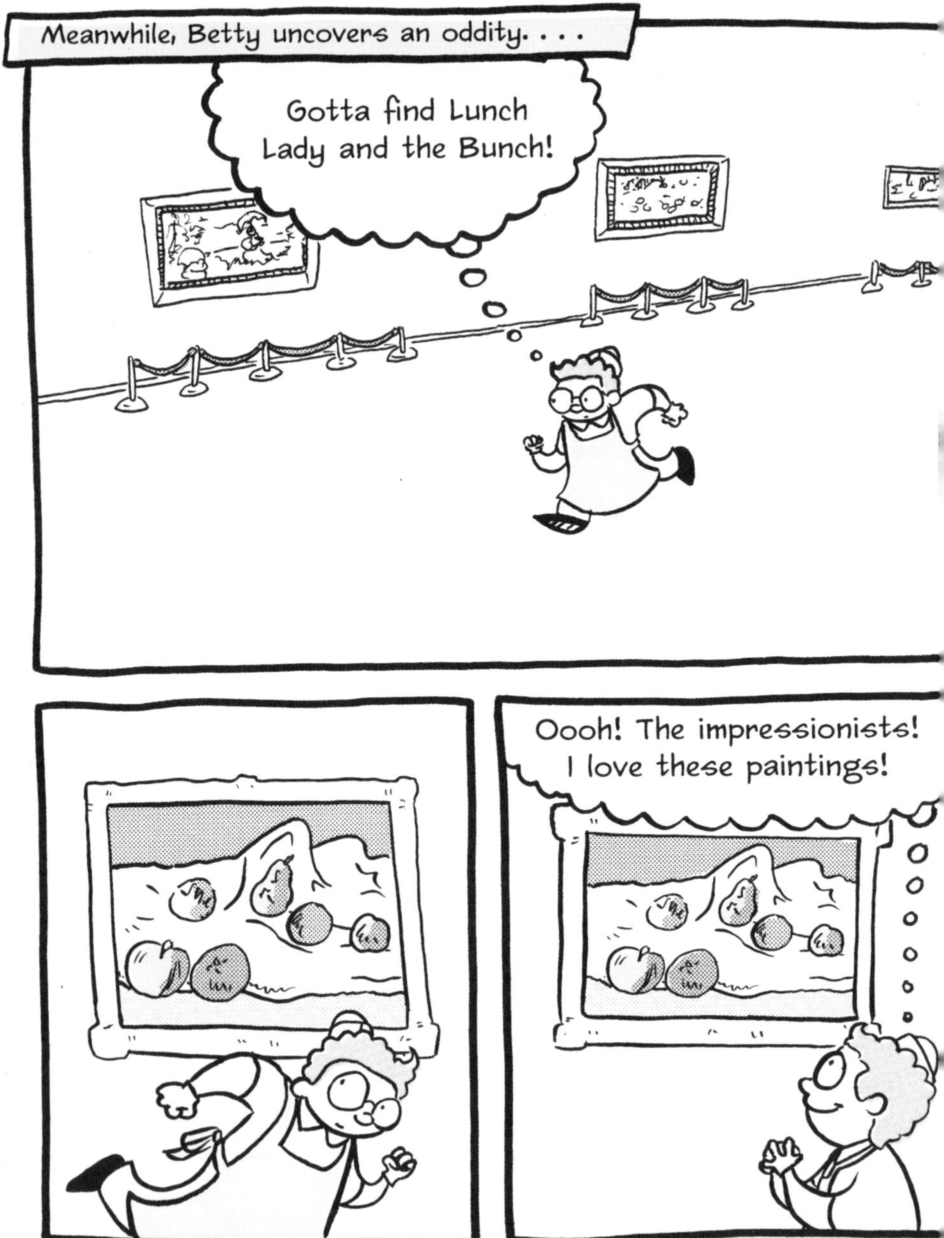
Meanwhile, Betty uncovers an oddity. . . .
Gotta find Lunch Lady and the Bunch!
Oooh! The impressionists! I love these paintings!

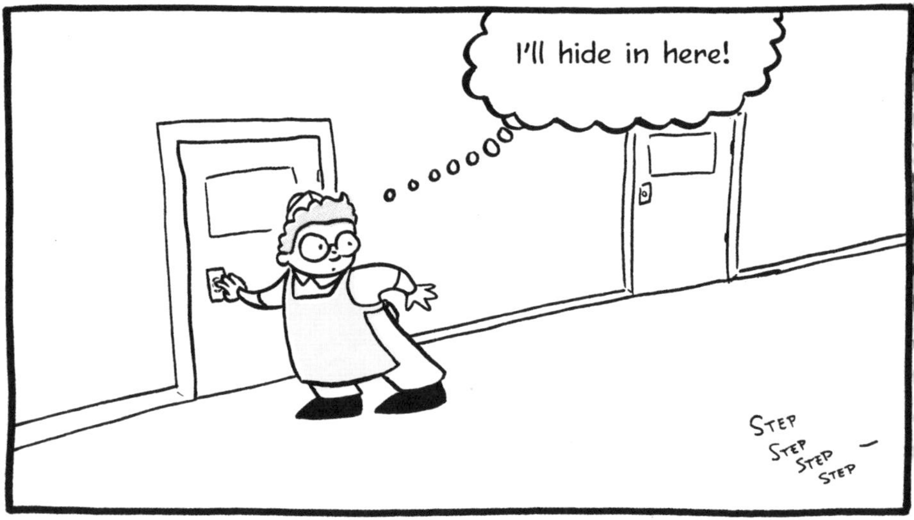
I'll hide in here!
STEP STEP STEP STEP

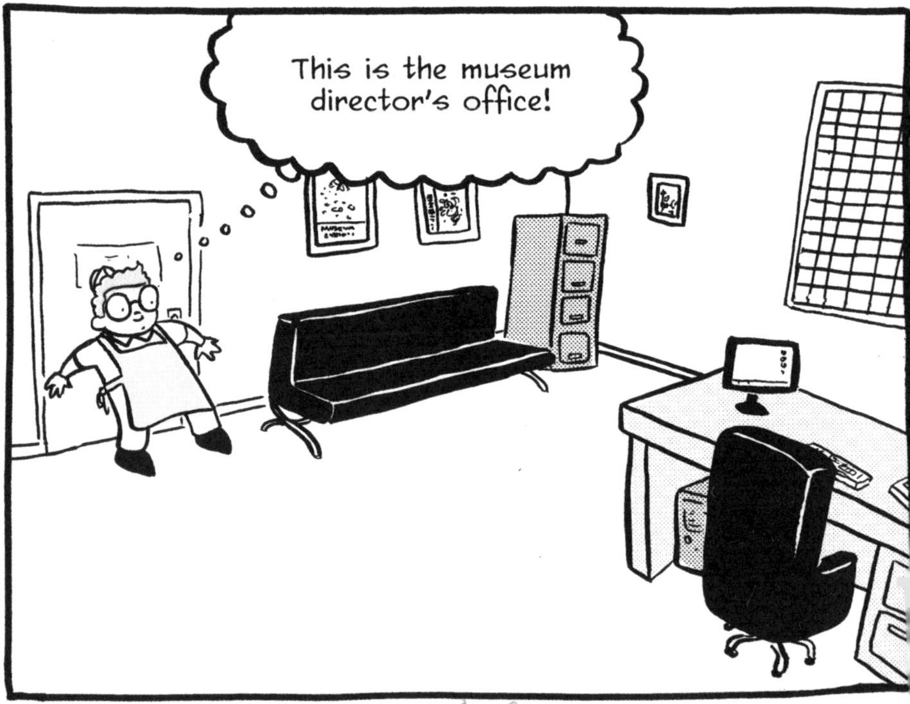
This is the museum director's office!

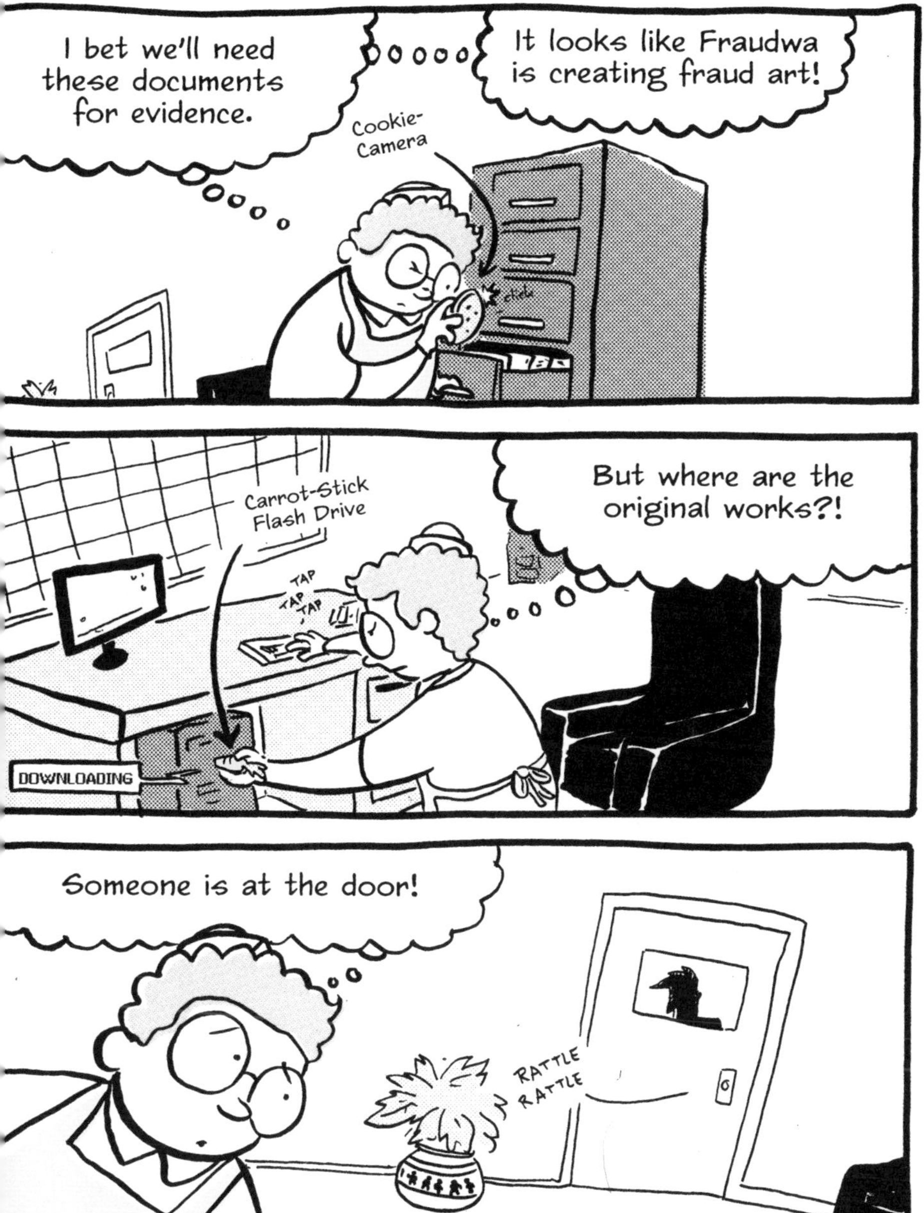
I bet we'll need these documents for evidence.
It looks like Fraudwa is creating fraud art!
Cookie-Camera
Carrot-Stick Flash Drive
TAP TAP TAP
DOWNLOADING
But where are the original works?!
Someone is at the door!
RATTLE RATTLE

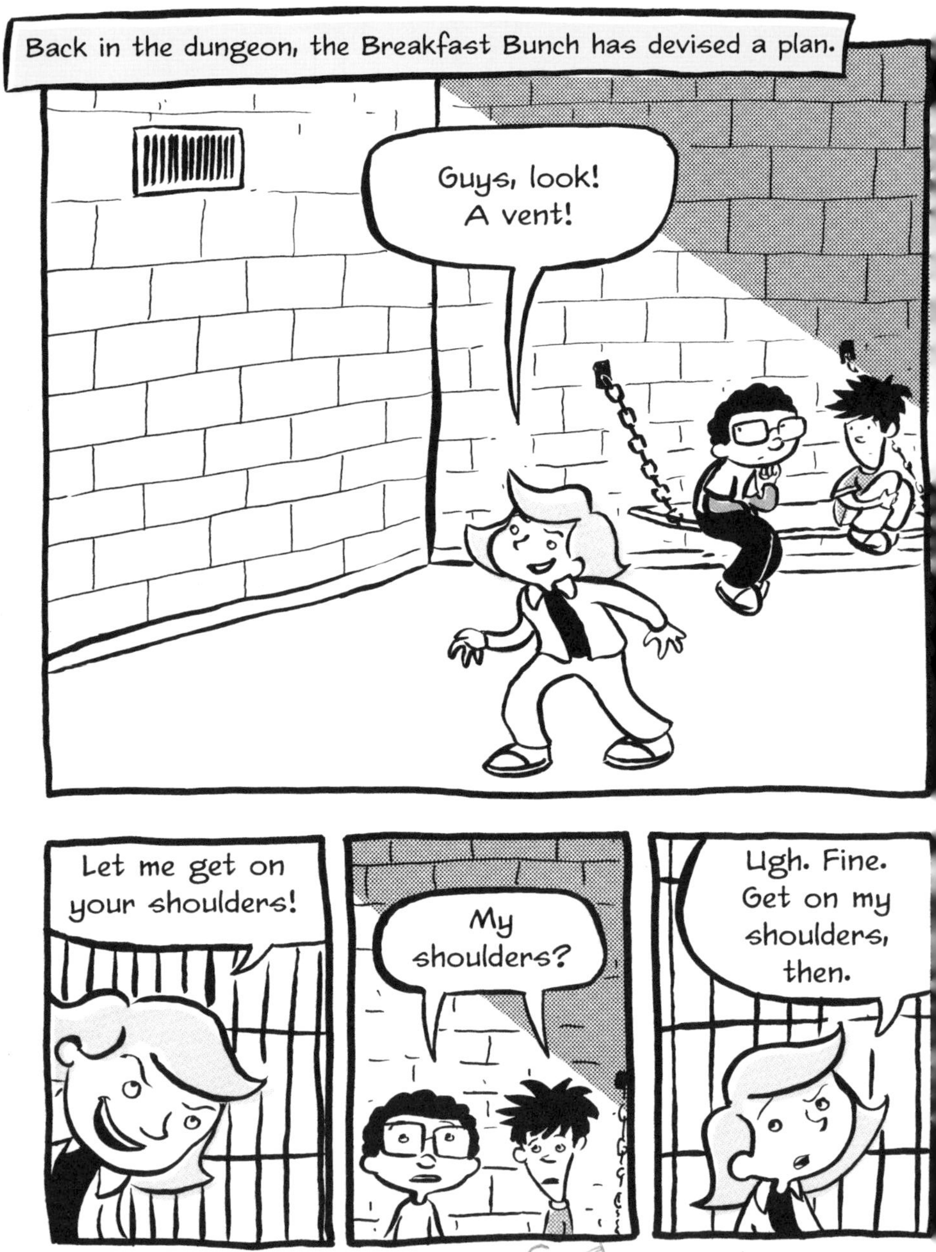
Back in the dungeon, the Breakfast Bunch has devised a plan.
Guys, look! A vent!
Let me get on your shoulders!
My shoulders?
Ugh. Fine. Get on my shoulders, then.

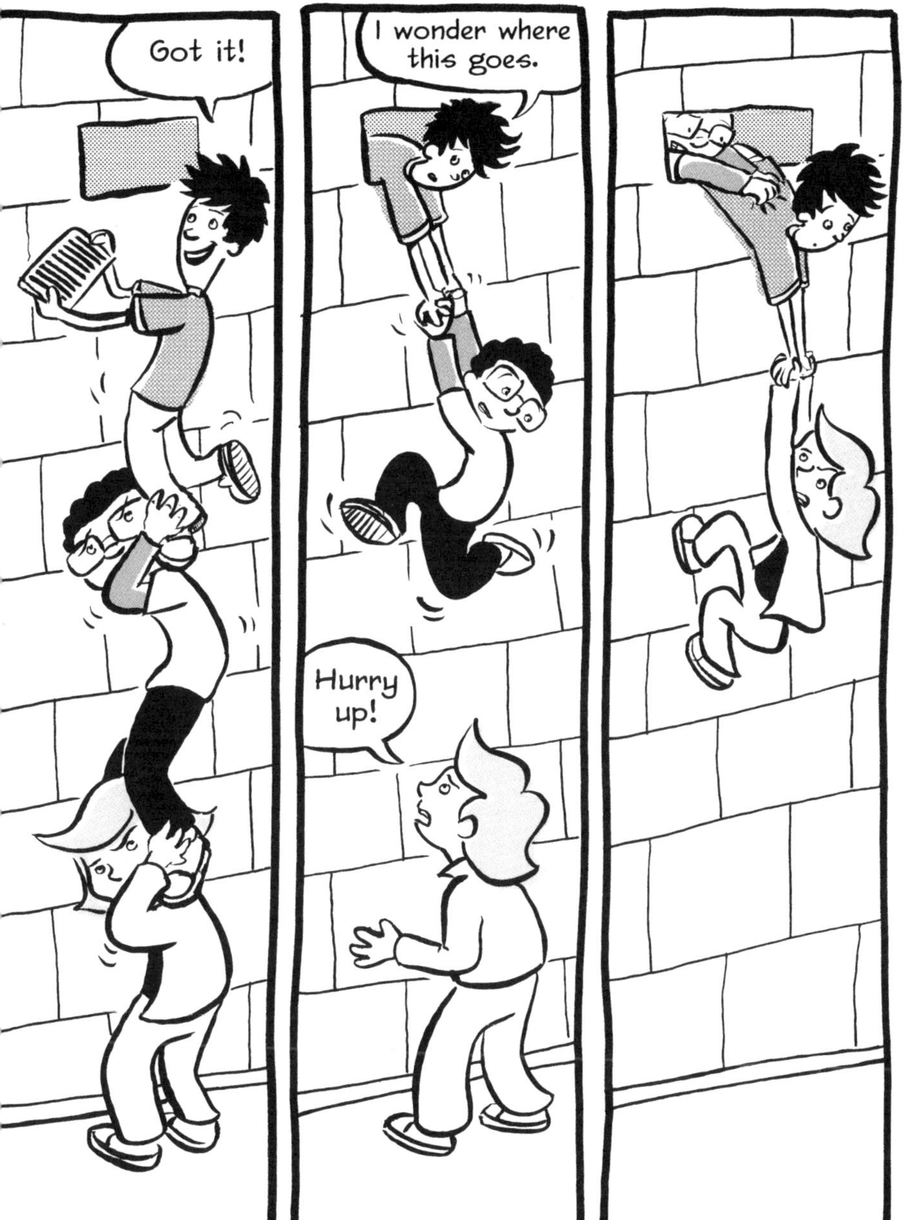
Got it!
I wonder where this goes.
Hurry up!

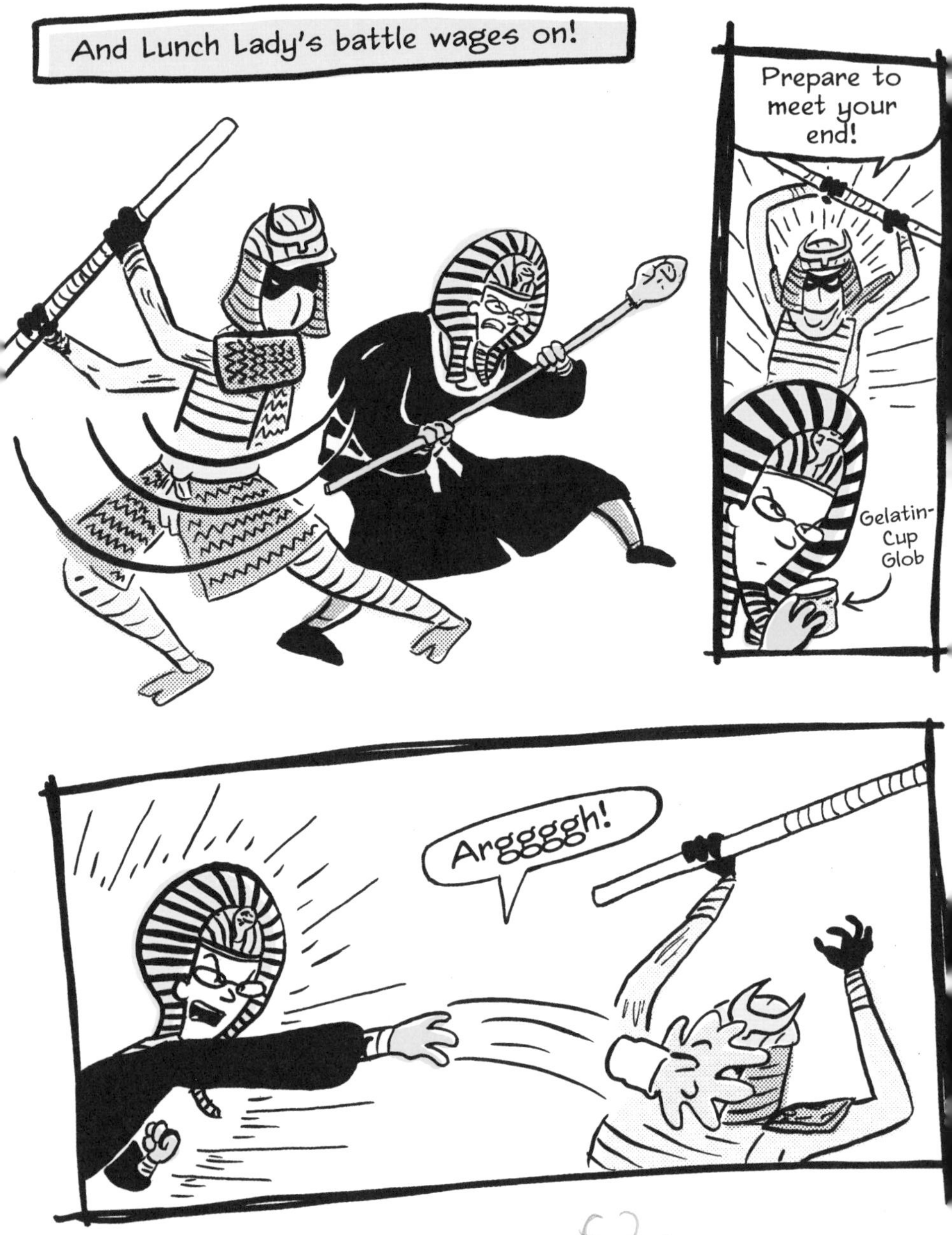

And Lunch Lady's battle wages on!
Prepare to meet your end!
Gelatin-Cup Glob
Argggggh!

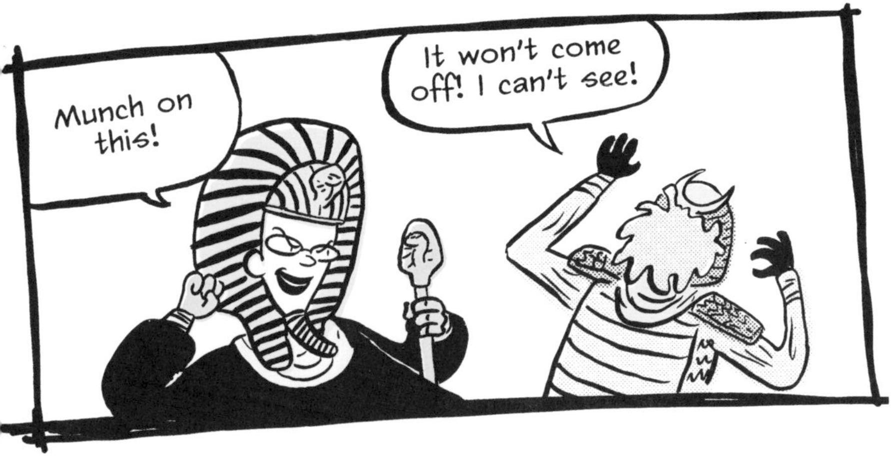
Munch on this!
It won't come off! I can't see!

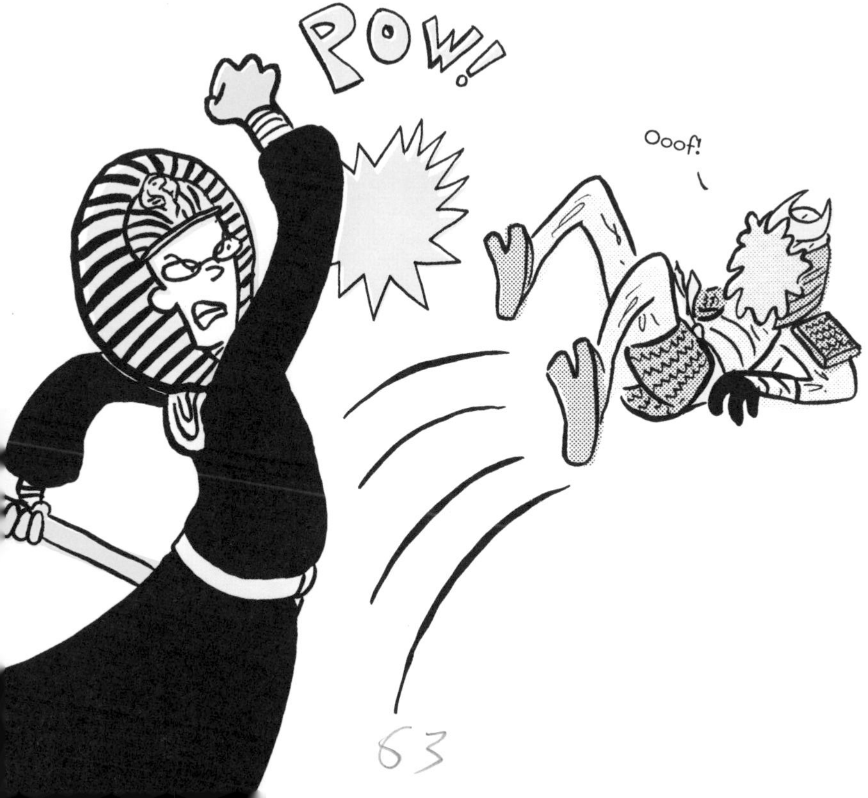
POW!
Ooof!

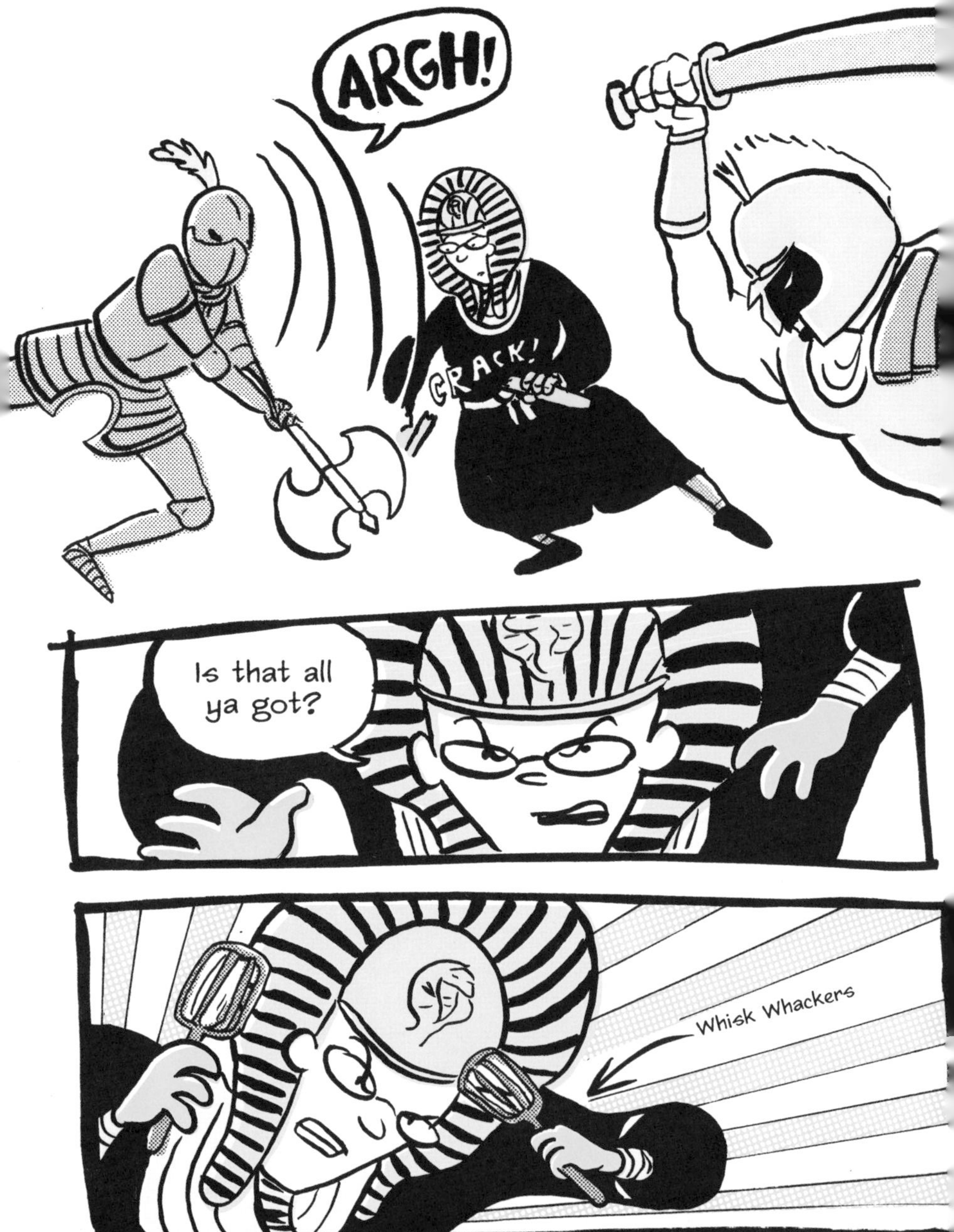
ARGH!
CRACK!
Is that all ya got?
Whisk Whackers

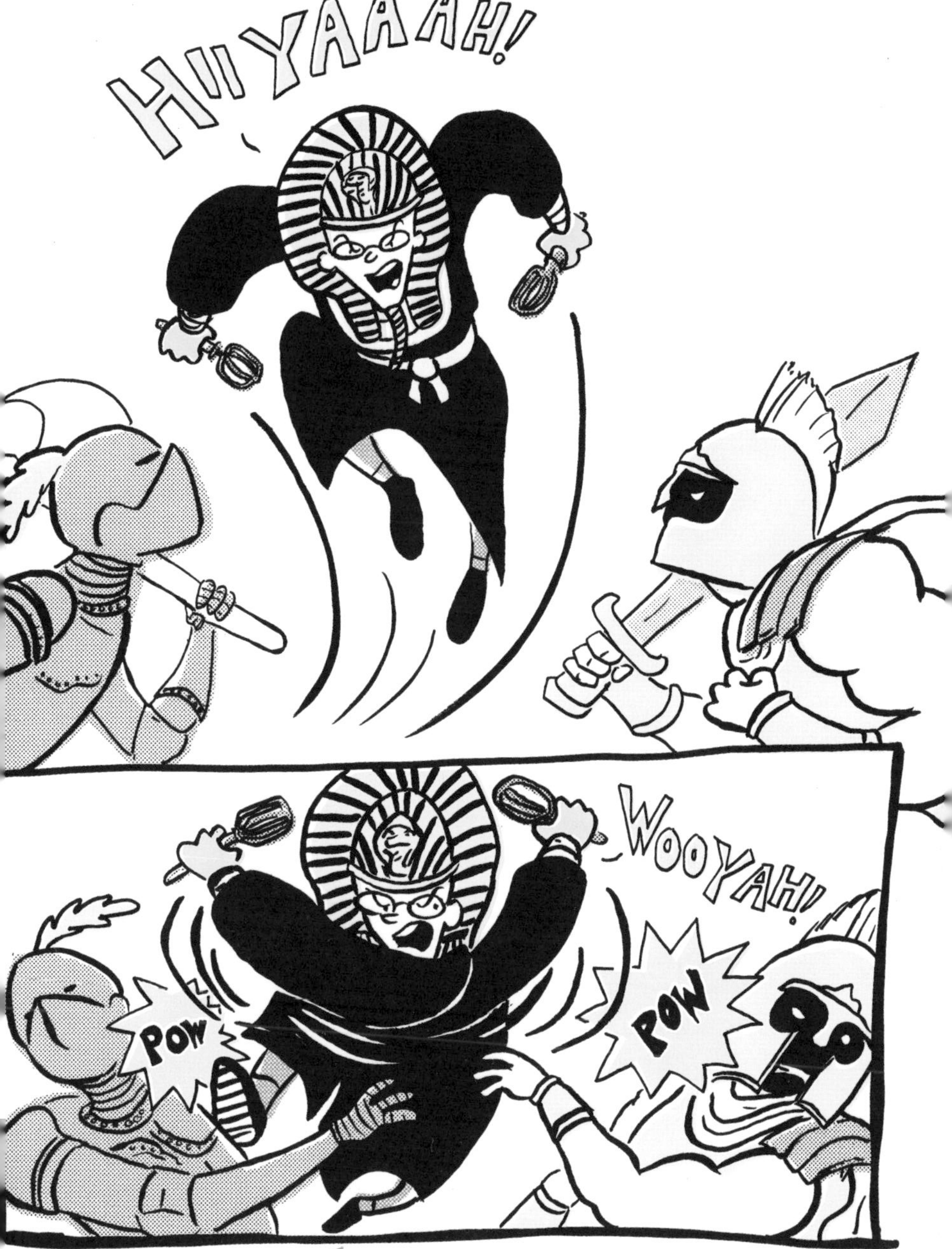
HIIYAAAH!
WOOYAH!
POW
POW

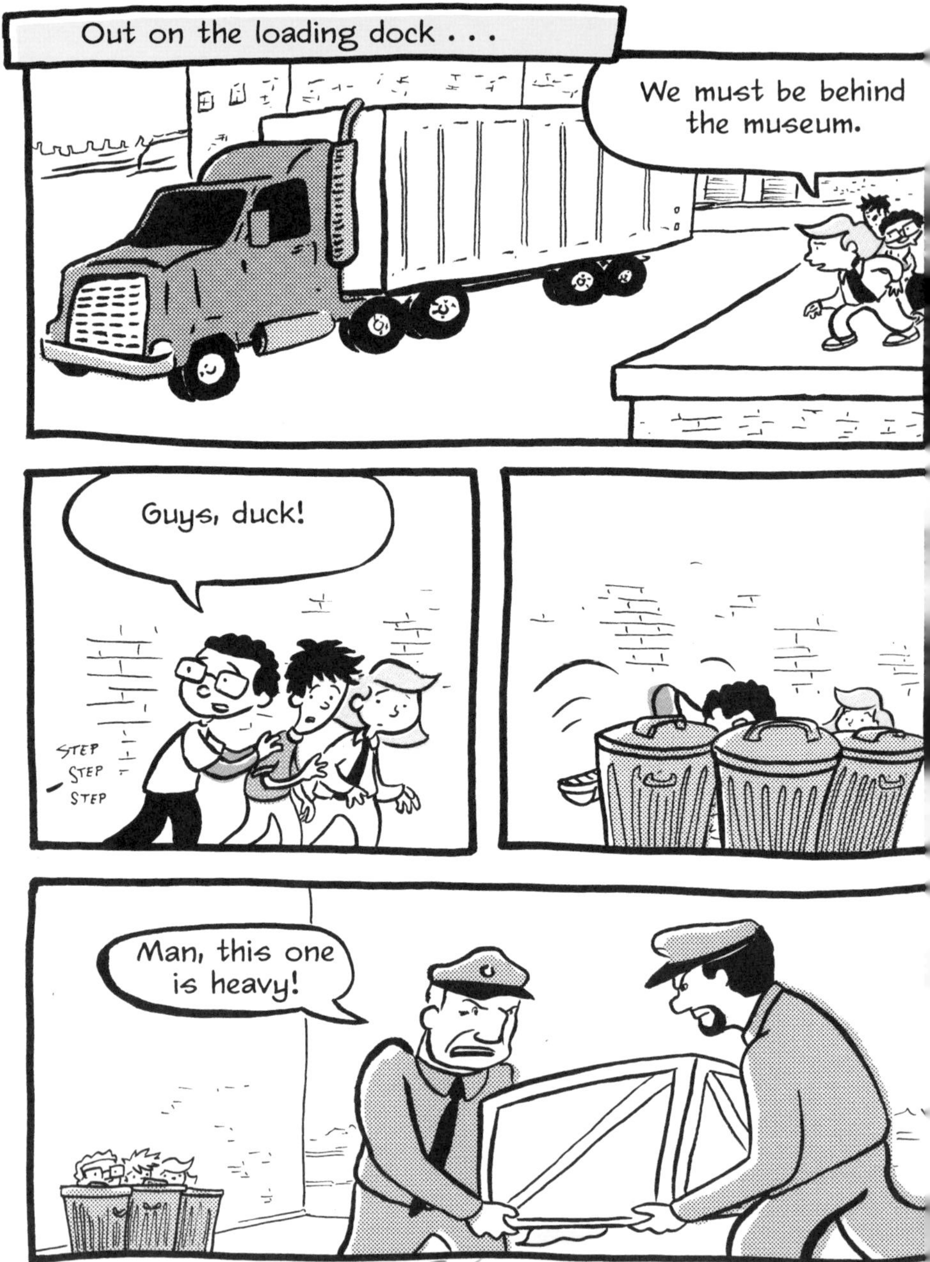
Out on the loading dock . . .
We must be behind the museum.
Guys, duck!
STEP
STEP
STEP
Man, this one is heavy!

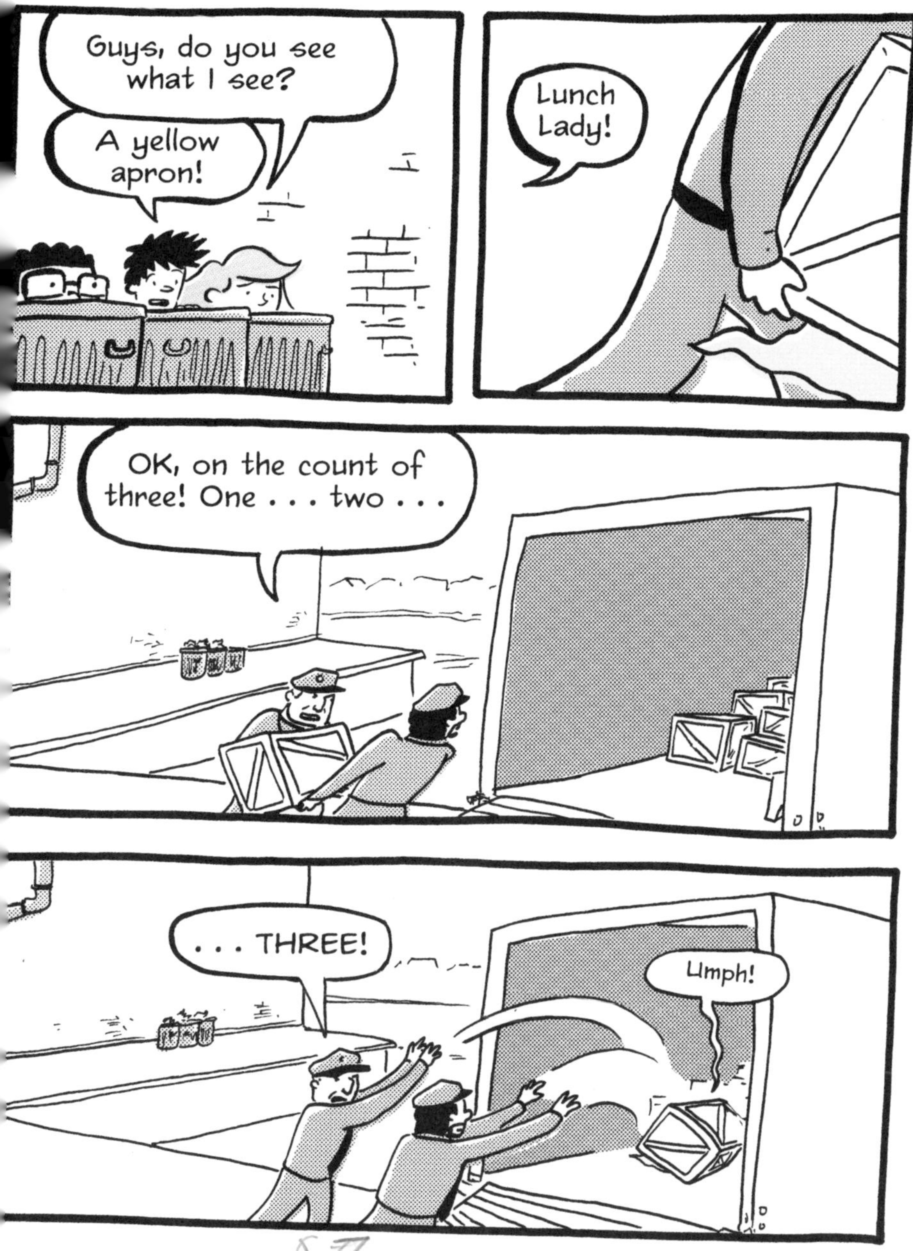
Guys, do you see what I see?
A yellow apron!
Lunch Lady!
OK, on the count of three! One . . . two . . .
. . . THREE!
Umph!

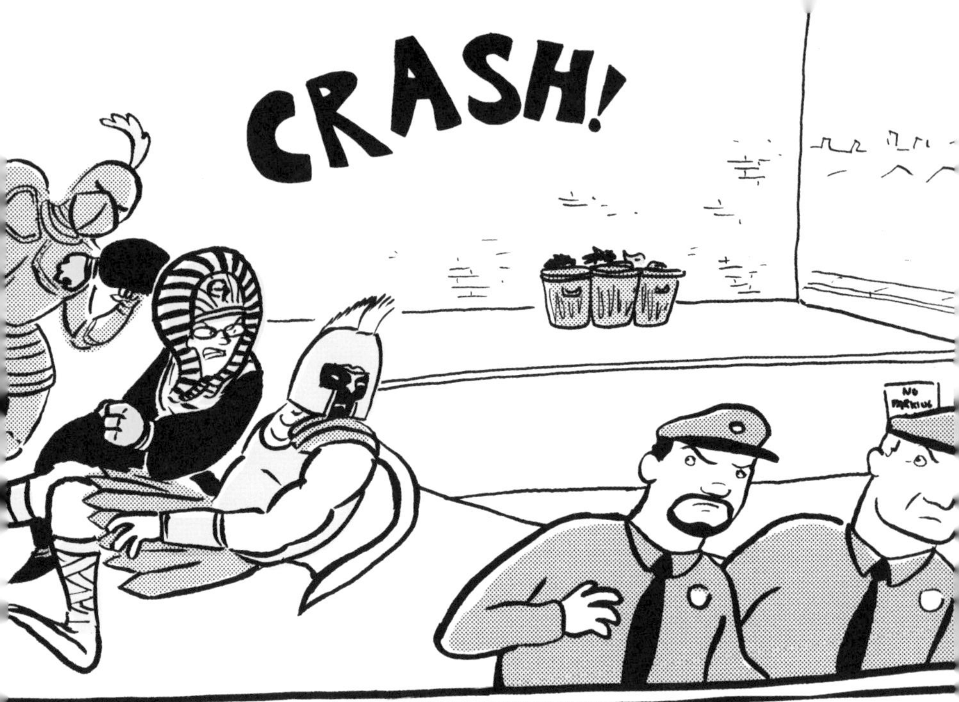
CRASH!
NO PARKING

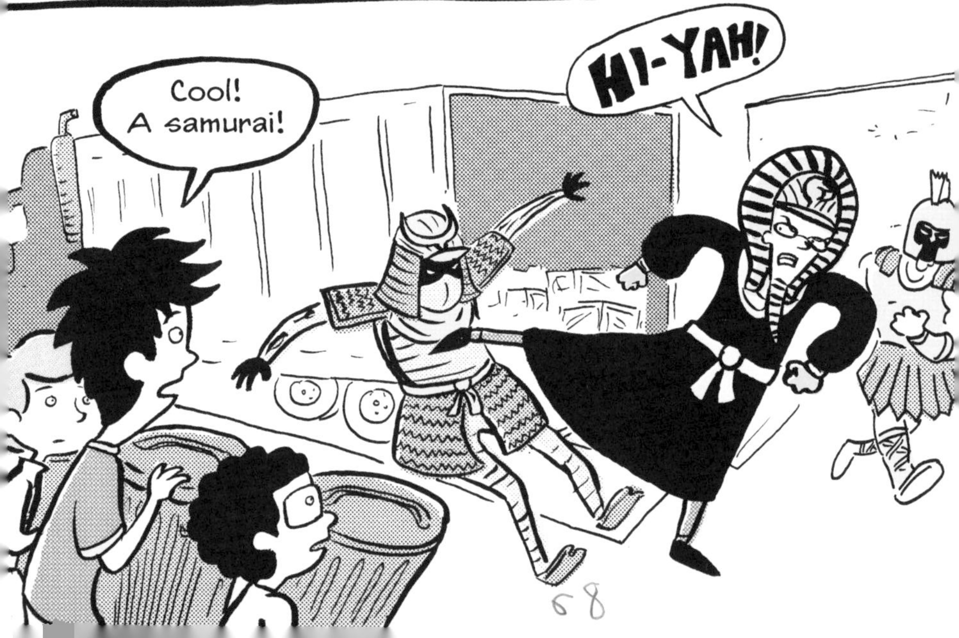
Cool! A samurai!
HI-YAH!

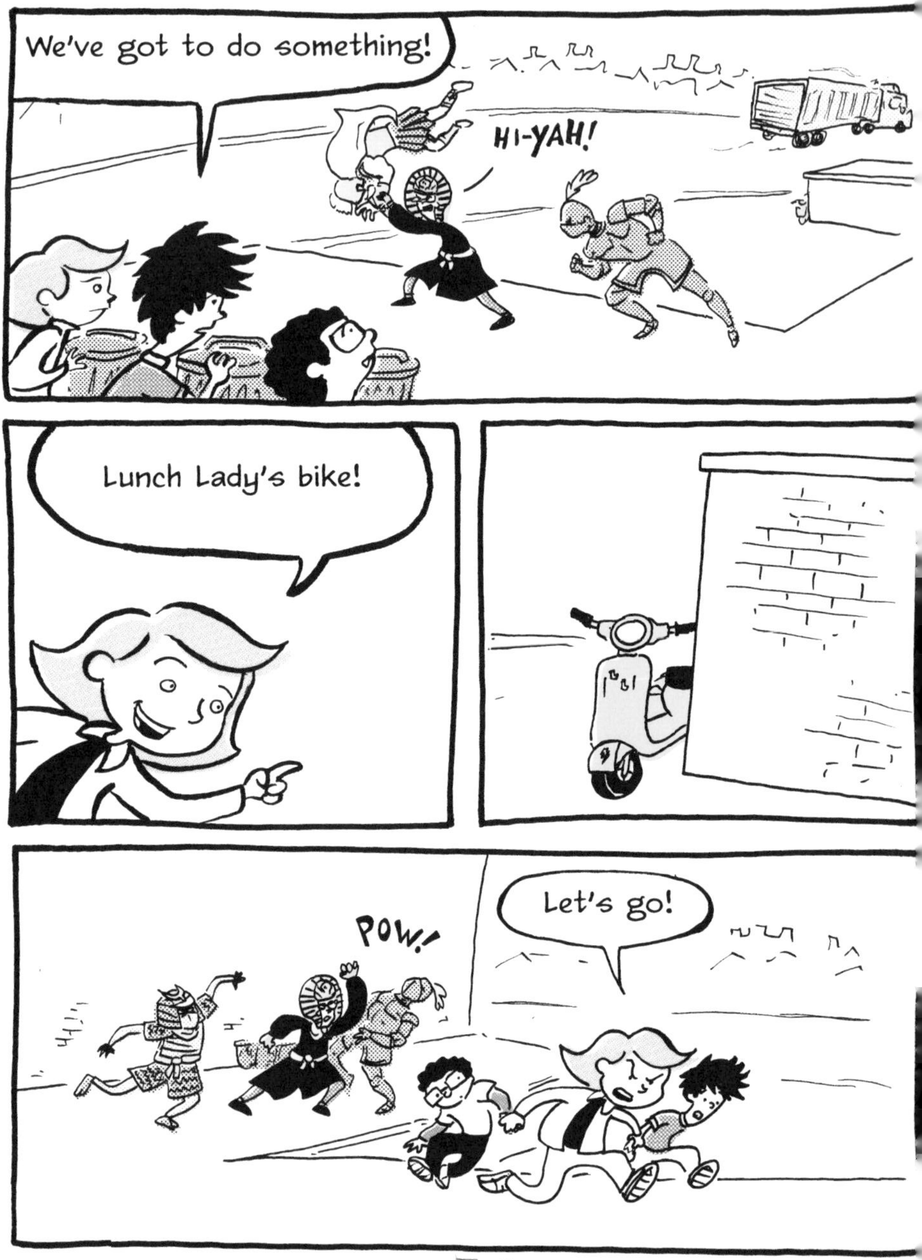
We've got to do something!
HI-YAH!
Lunch Lady's bike!
POW!
Let's go!

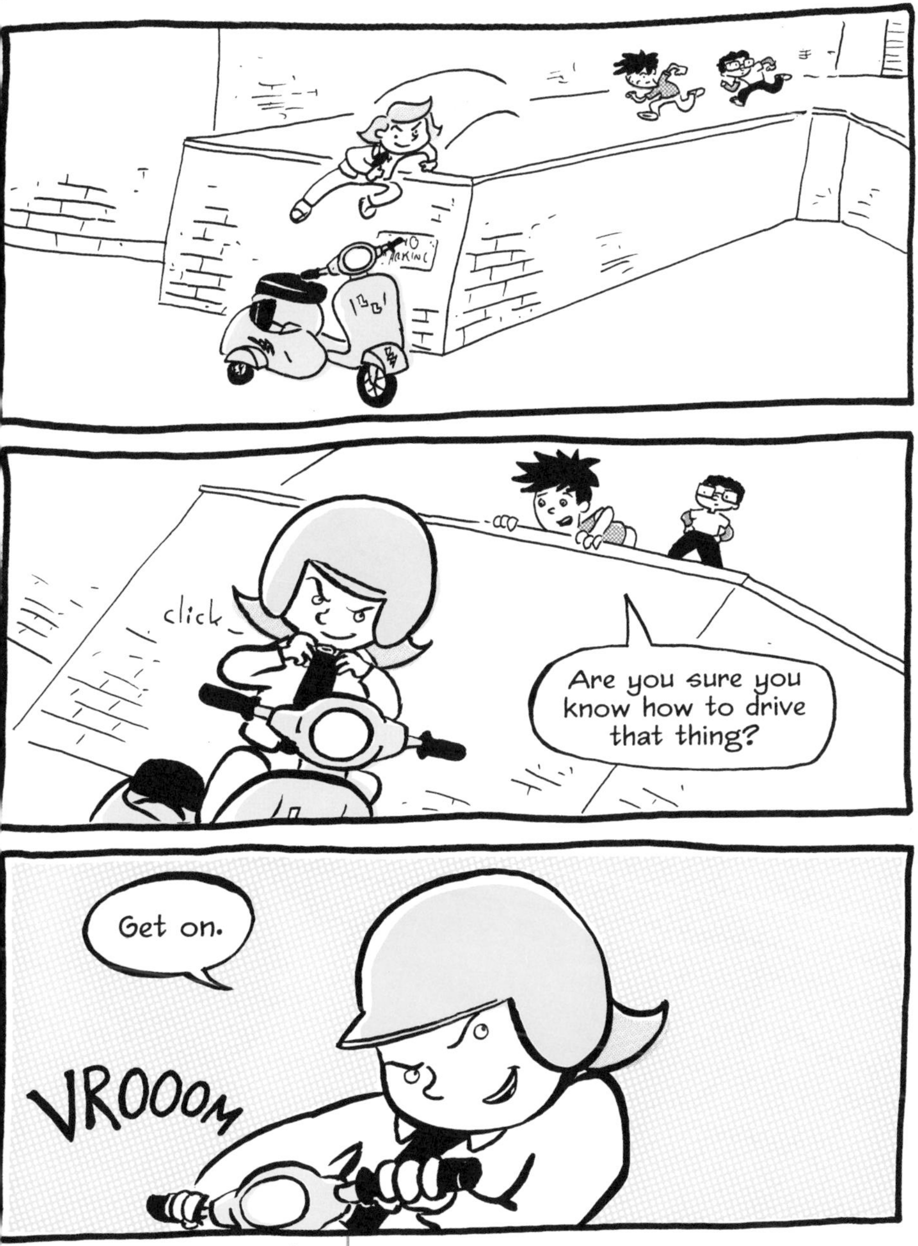
click
Are you sure you know how to drive that thing?
Get on.
VROOOM

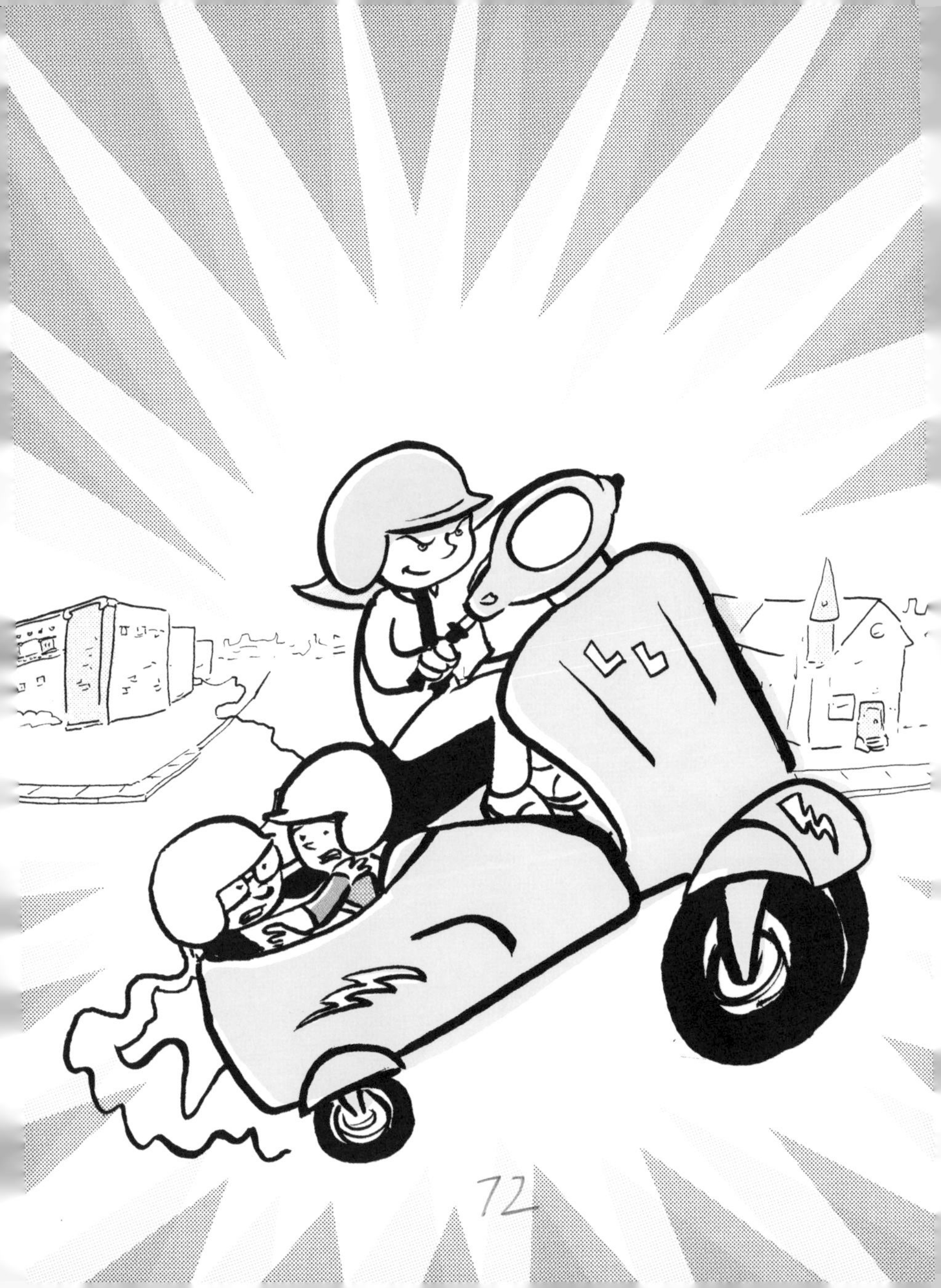

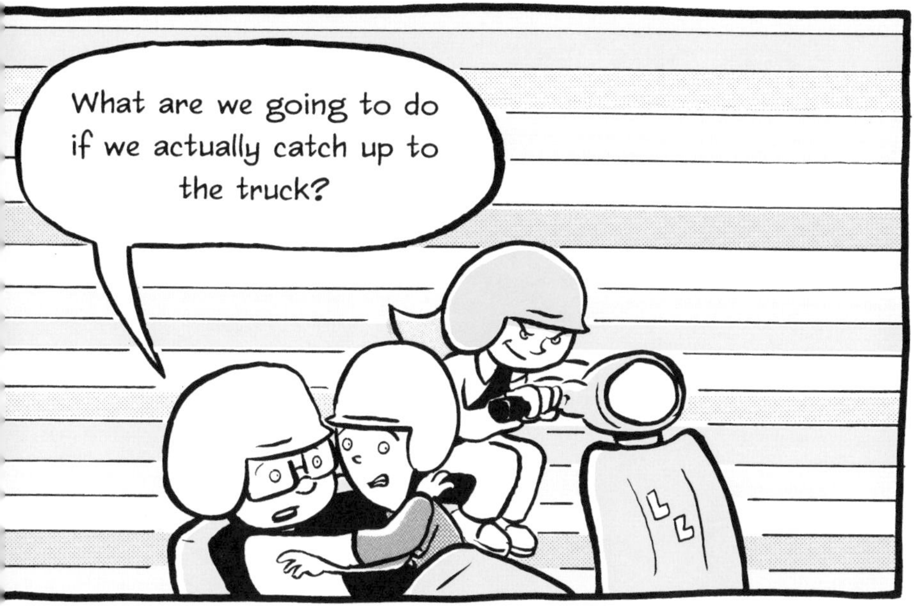
What are we going to do if we actually catch up to the truck?

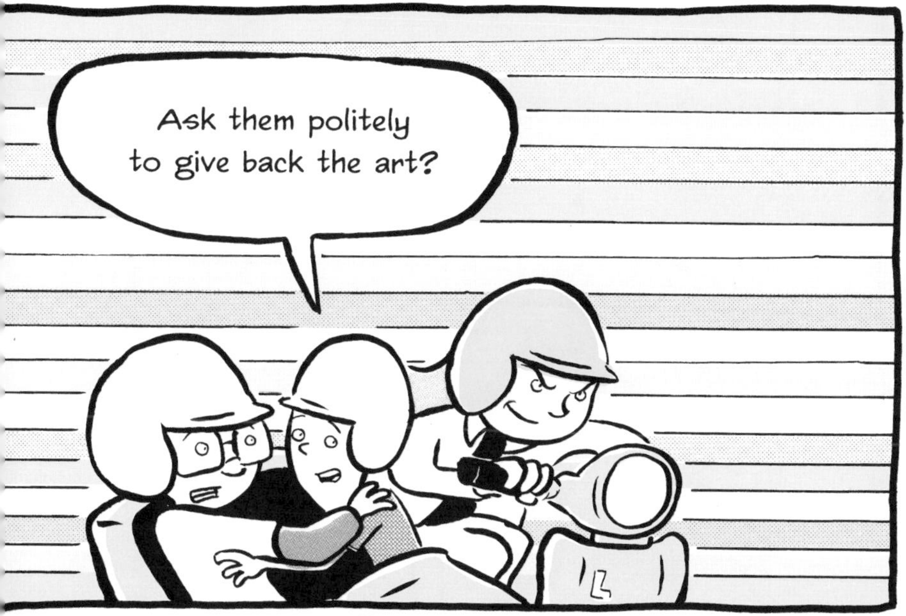
Ask them politely to give back the art?

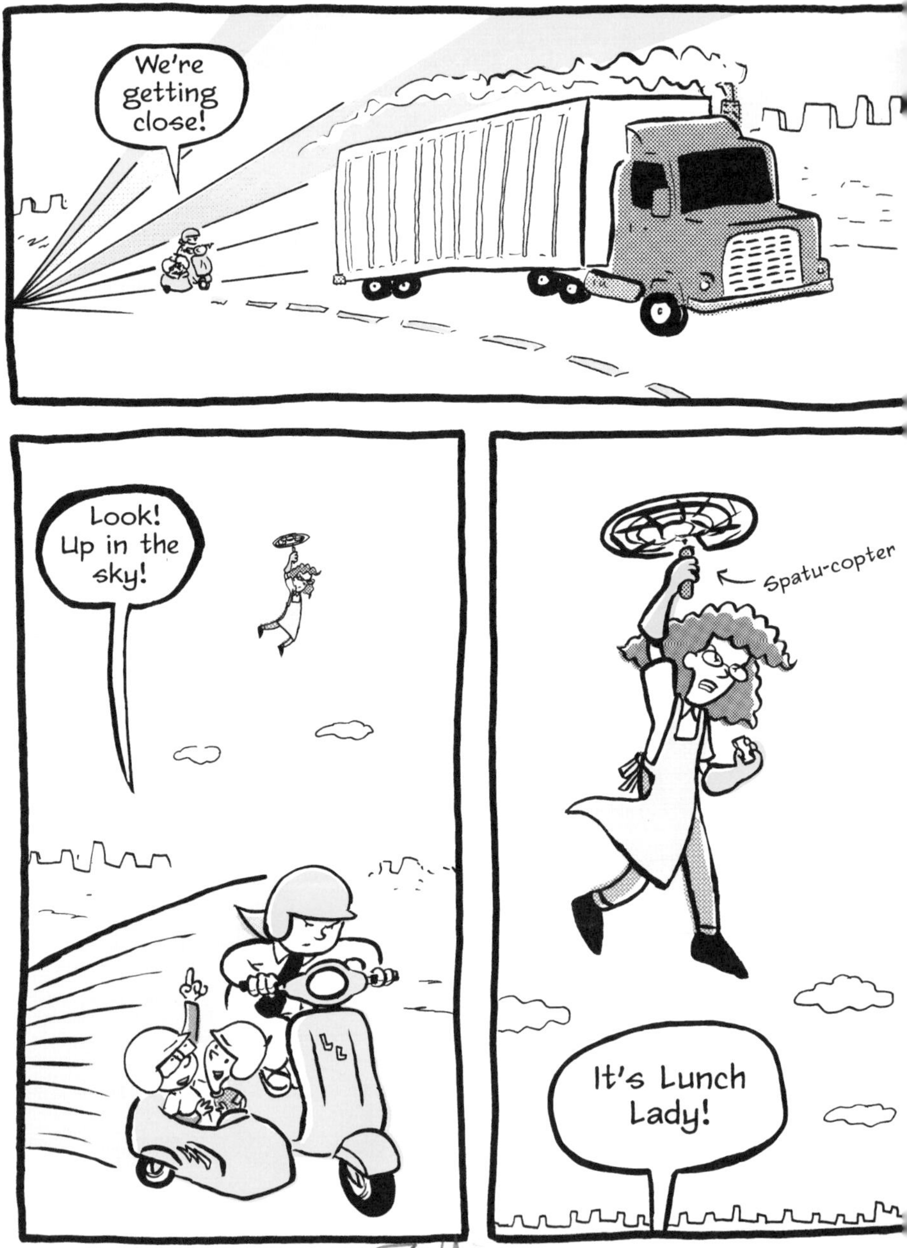
We're getting close!
Look! Up in the sky!
Spatu-copter
It's Lunch Lady!

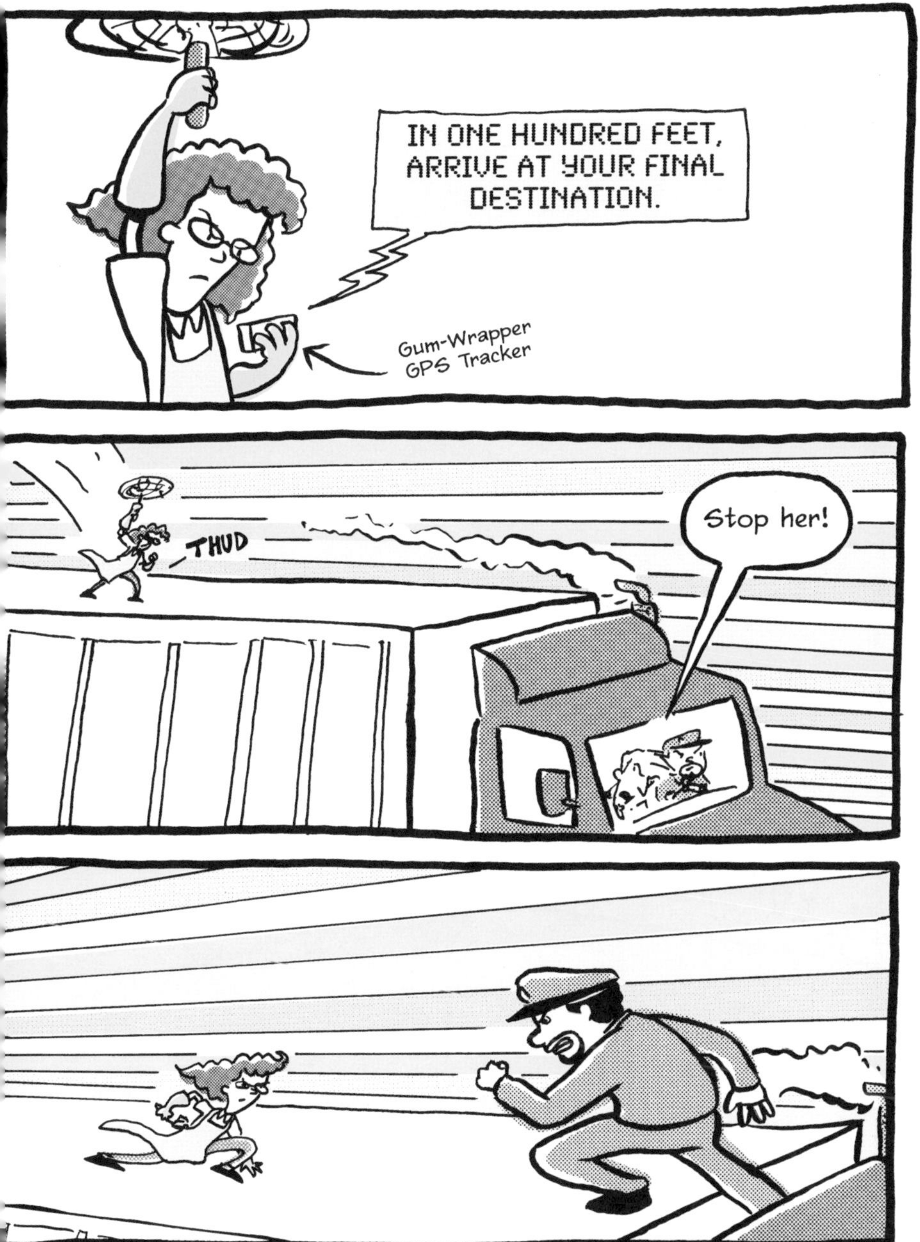
IN ONE HUNDRED FEET, ARRIVE AT YOUR FINAL DESTINATION.
Gum-Wrapper GPS Tracker
THUD
Stop her!

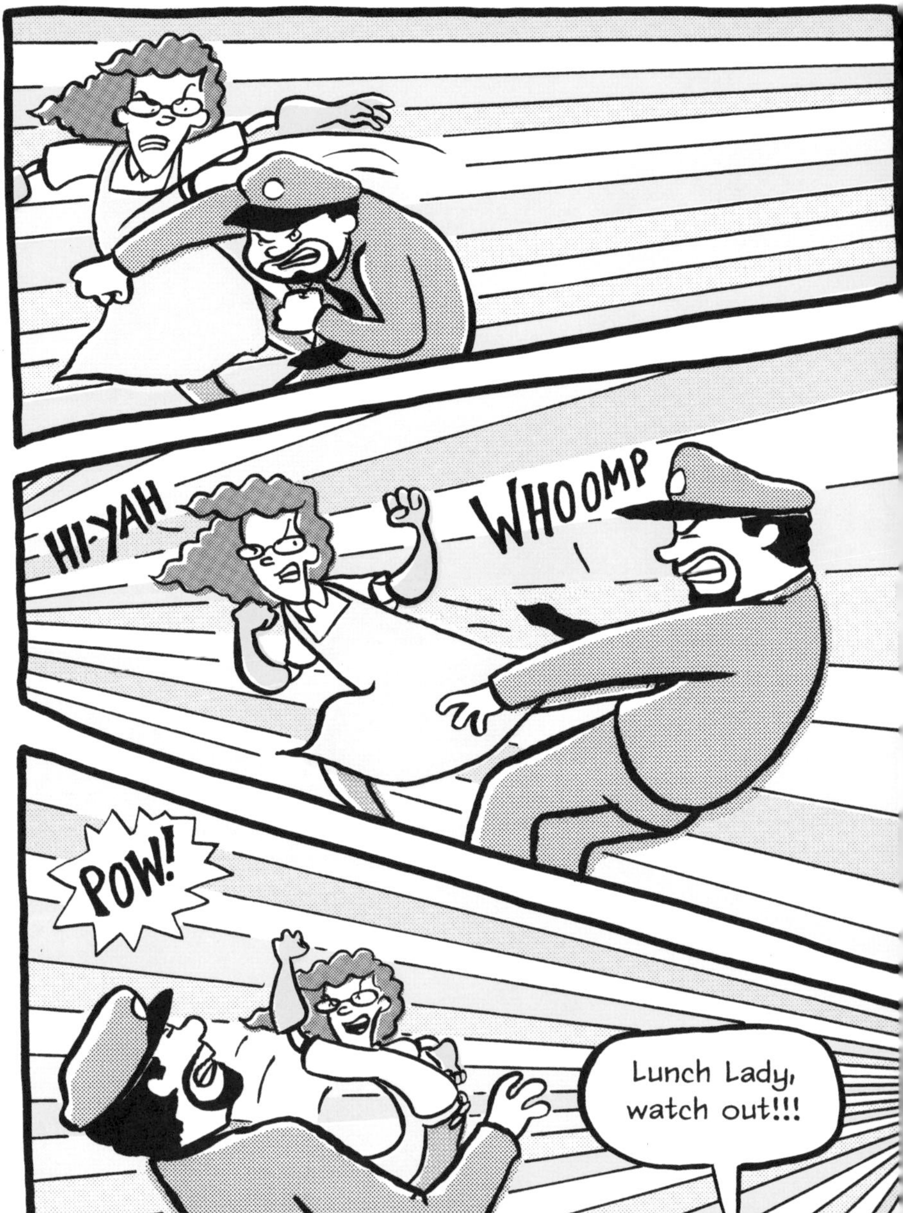
HI-YAH
WHOOMP
POW!
Lunch Lady, watch out!!!

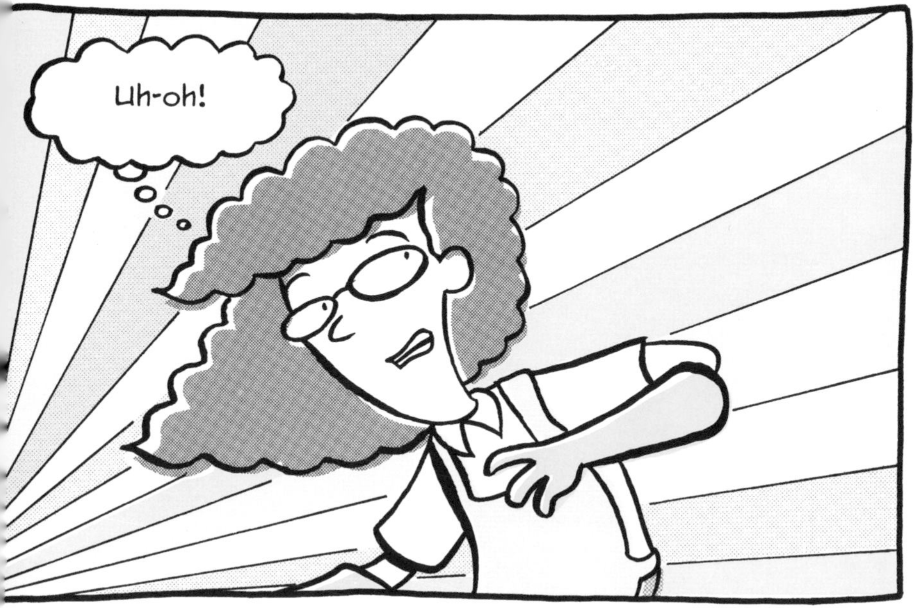
Uh-oh!

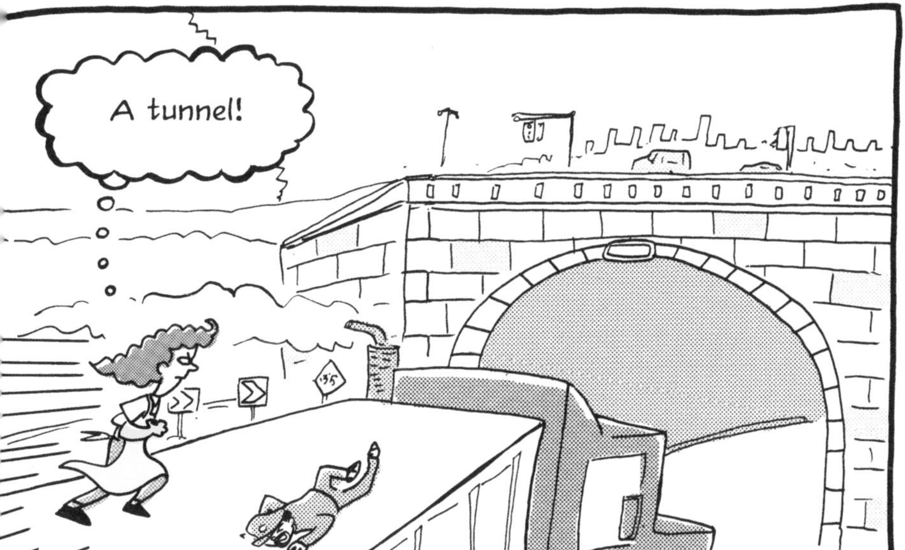
A tunnel!

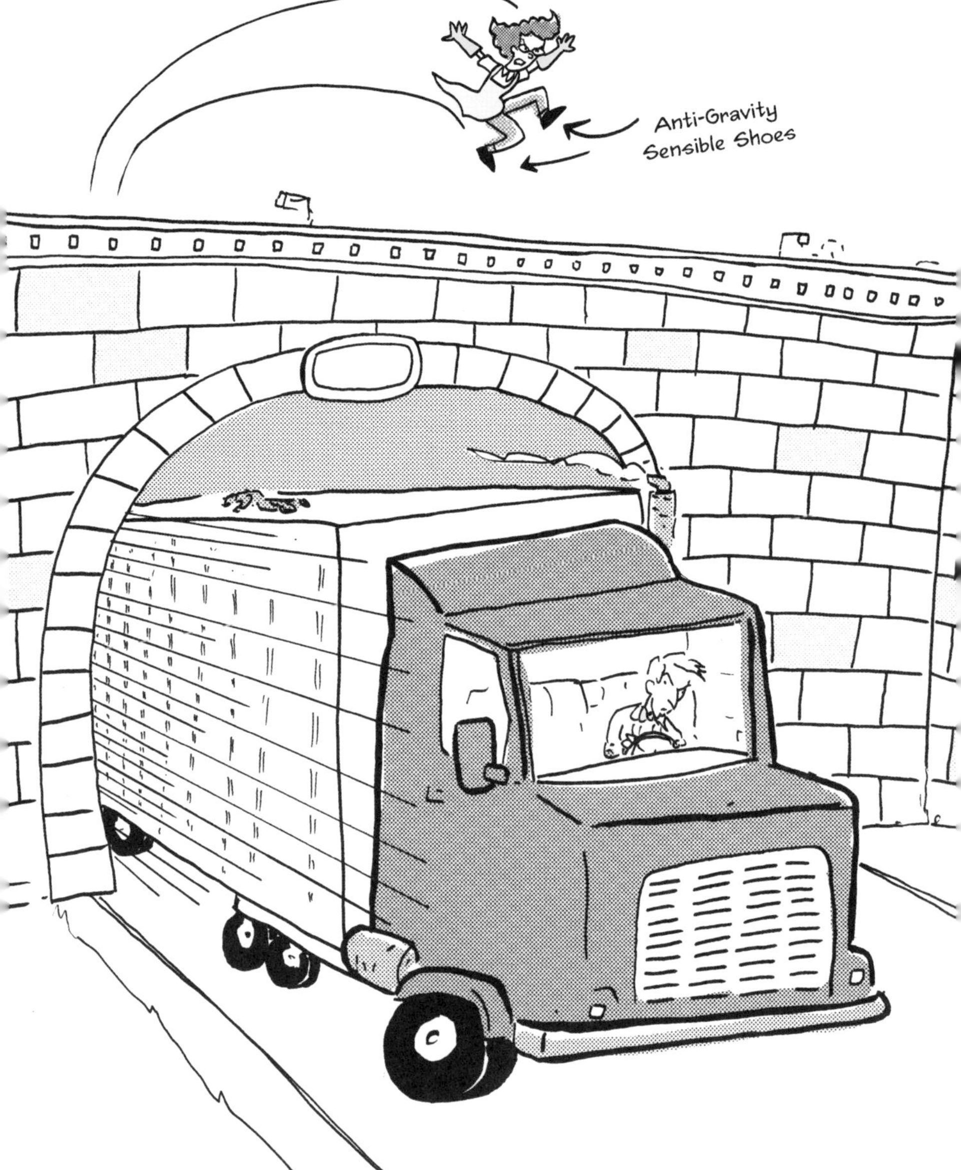
Anti-Gravity
Sensible Shoes

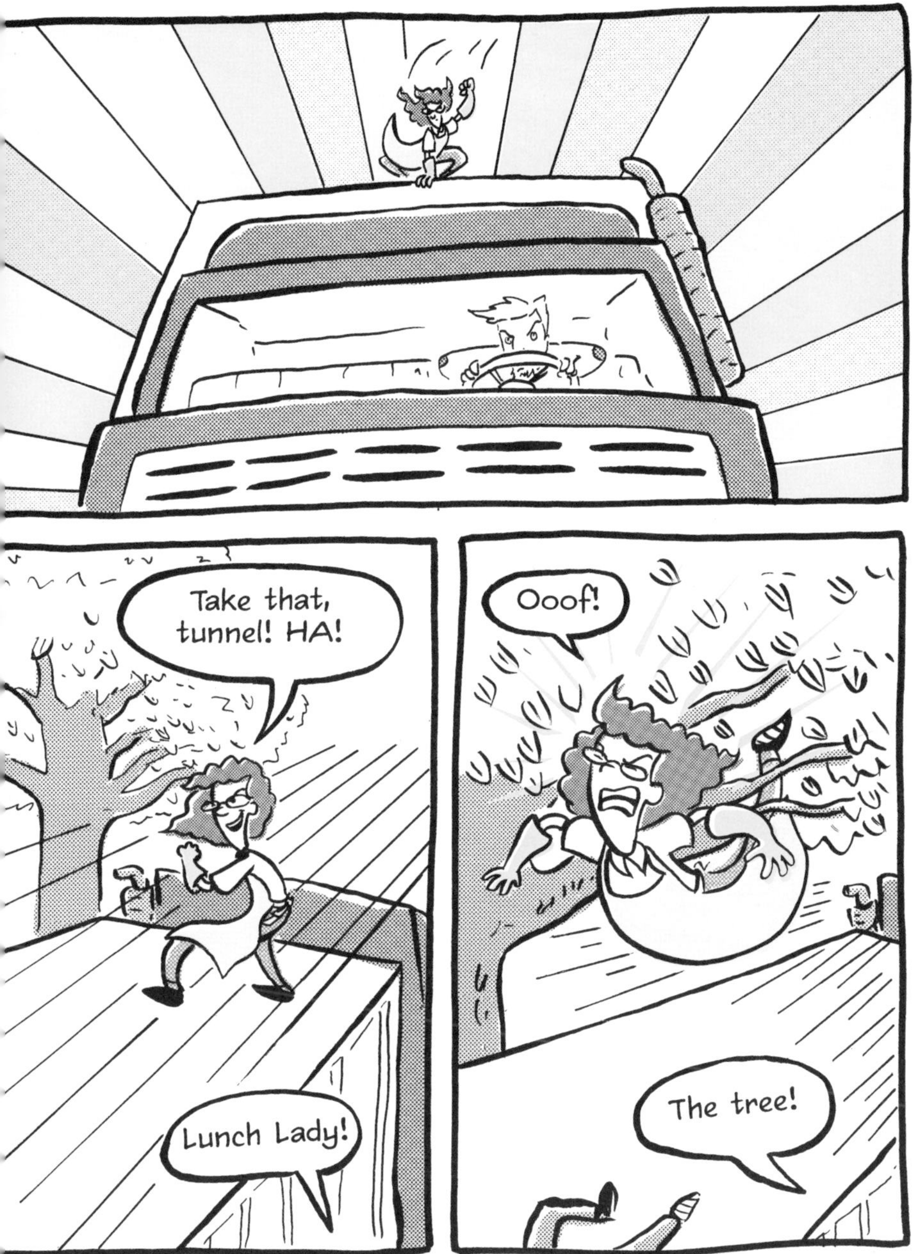
Take that, tunnel! HA!
Lunch Lady!
Ooof!
The tree!

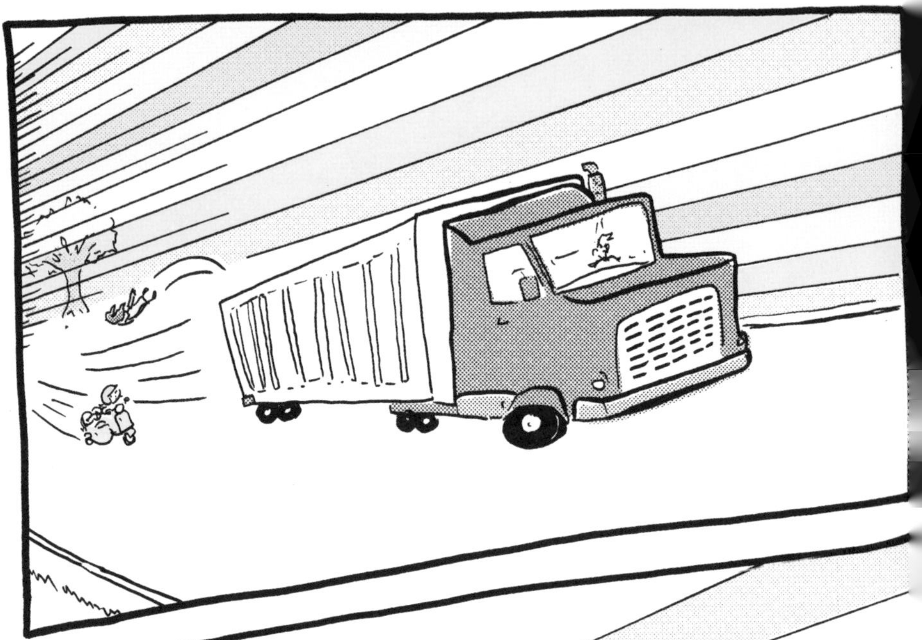

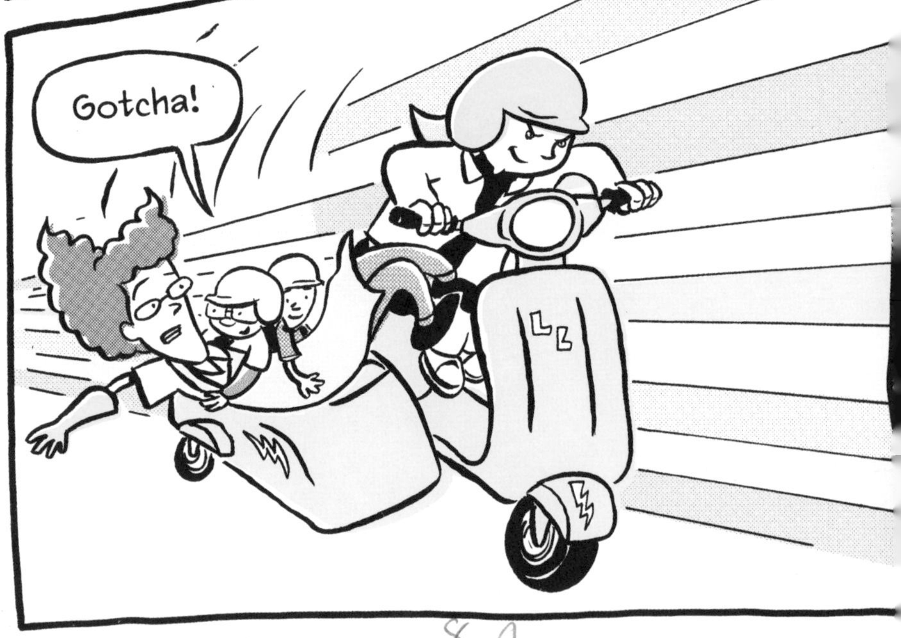
Gotcha!

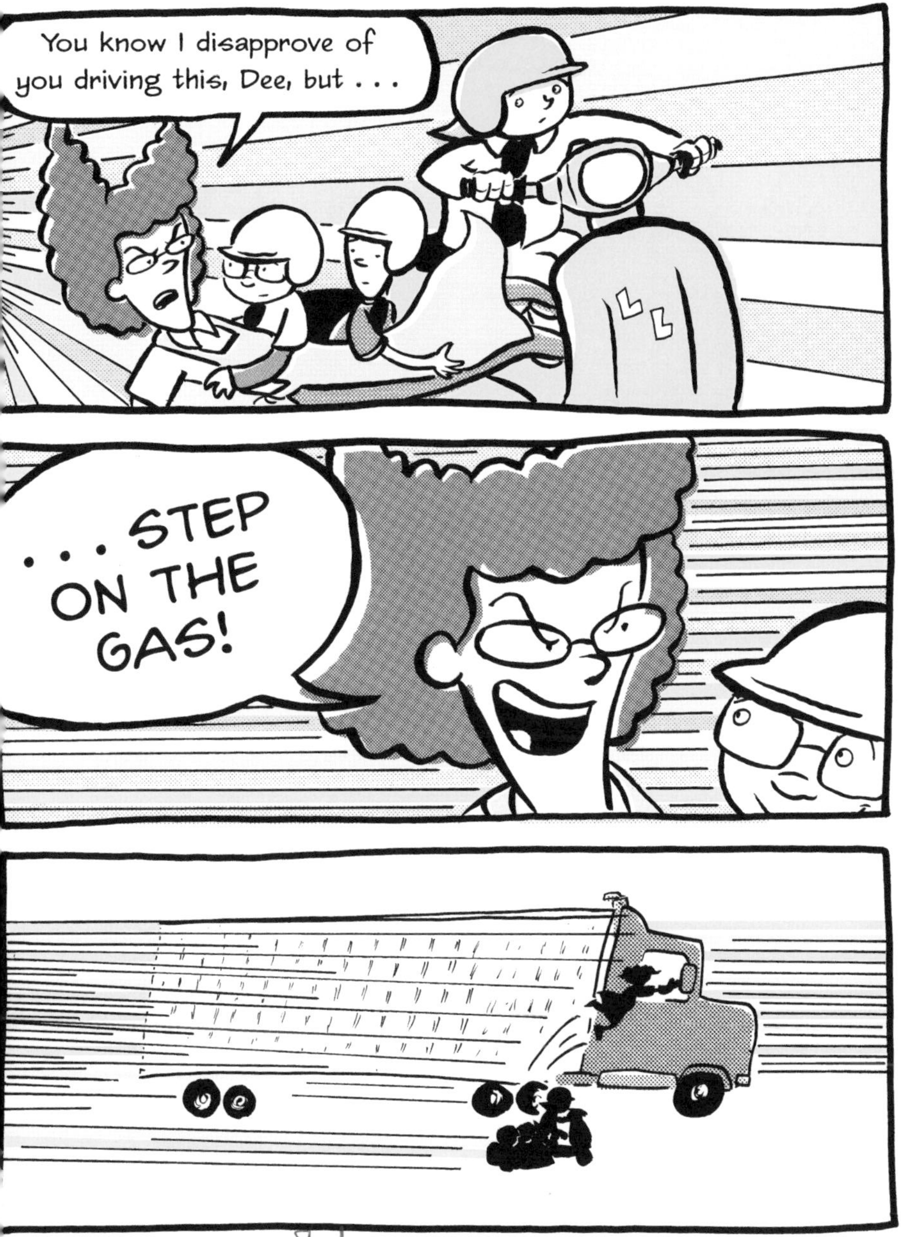
You know I disapprove of you driving this, Dee, but . . .
. . . STEP ON THE GAS!

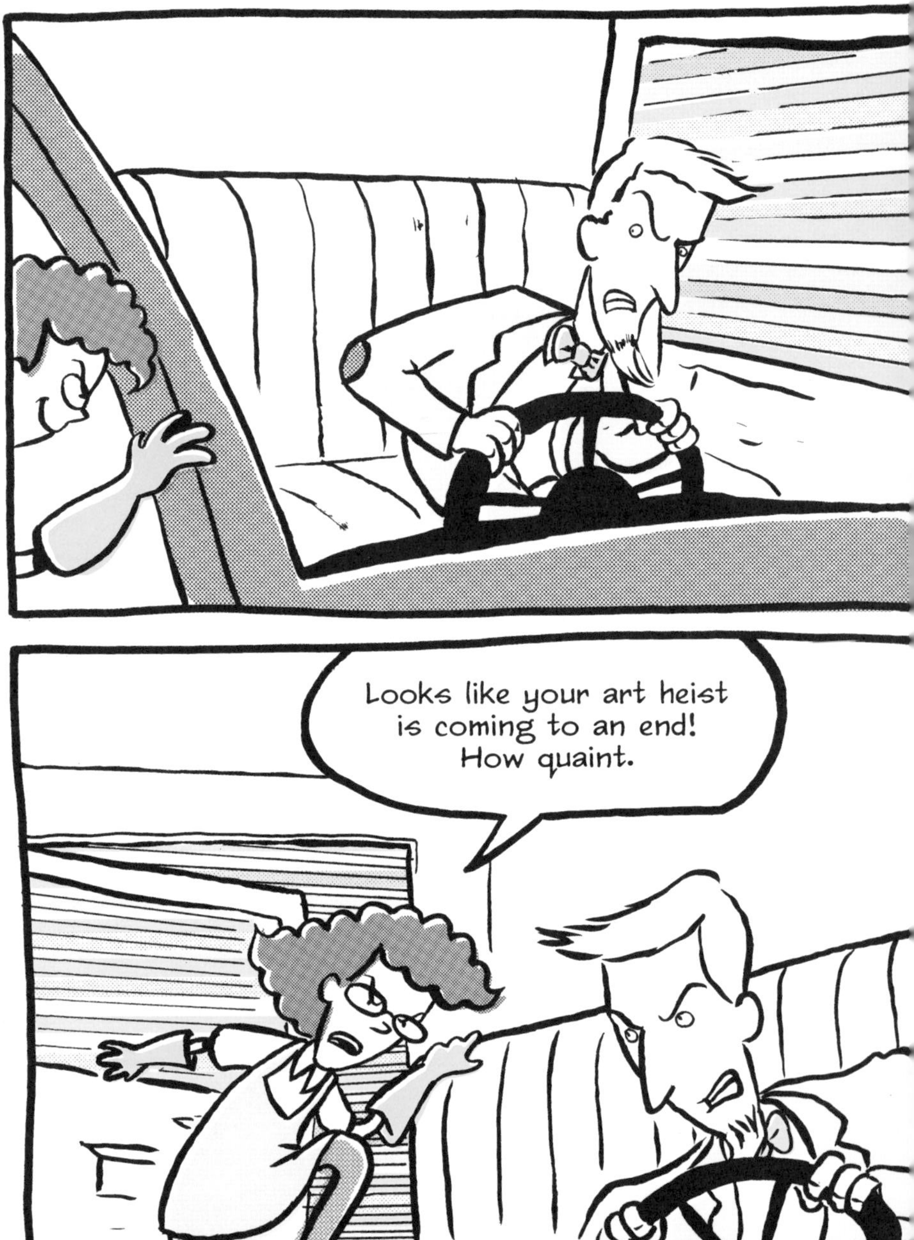
Looks like your art heist is coming to an end! How quaint.

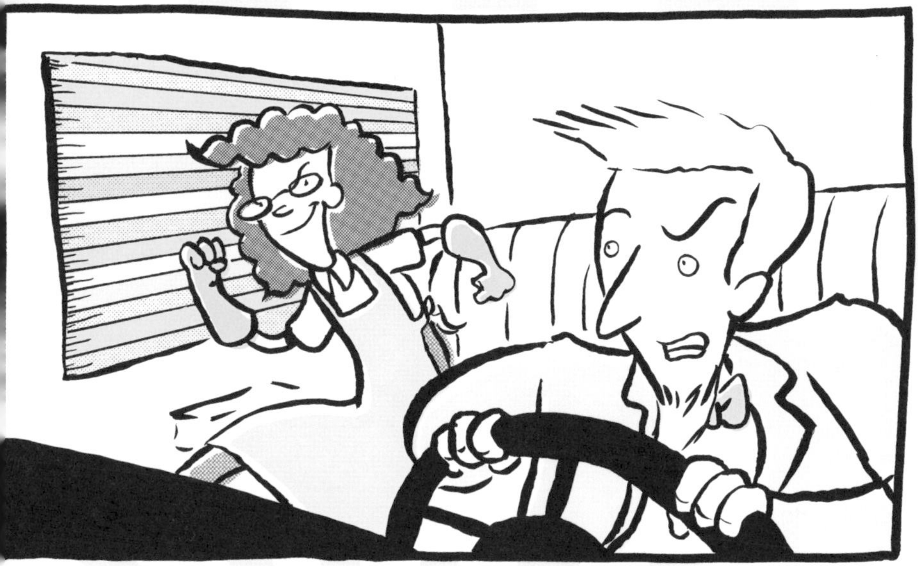

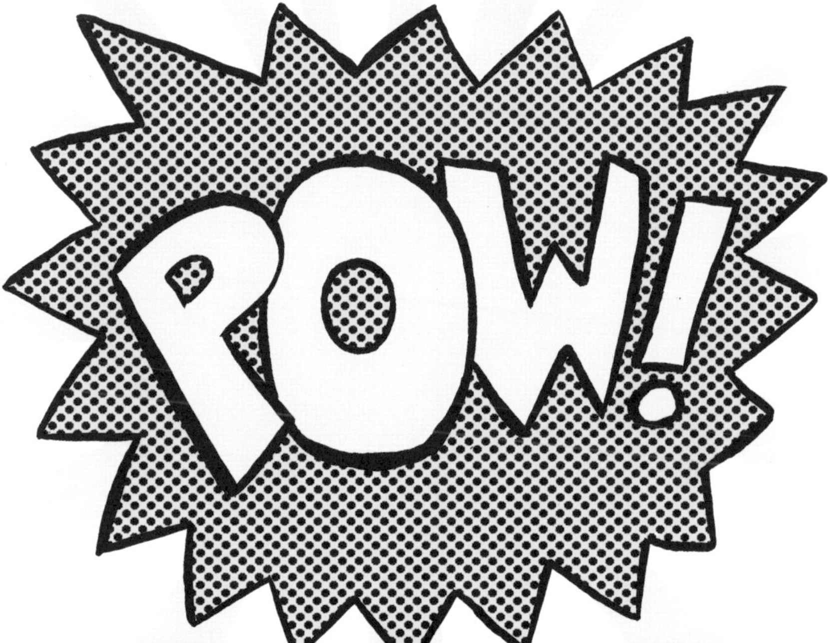
POW!

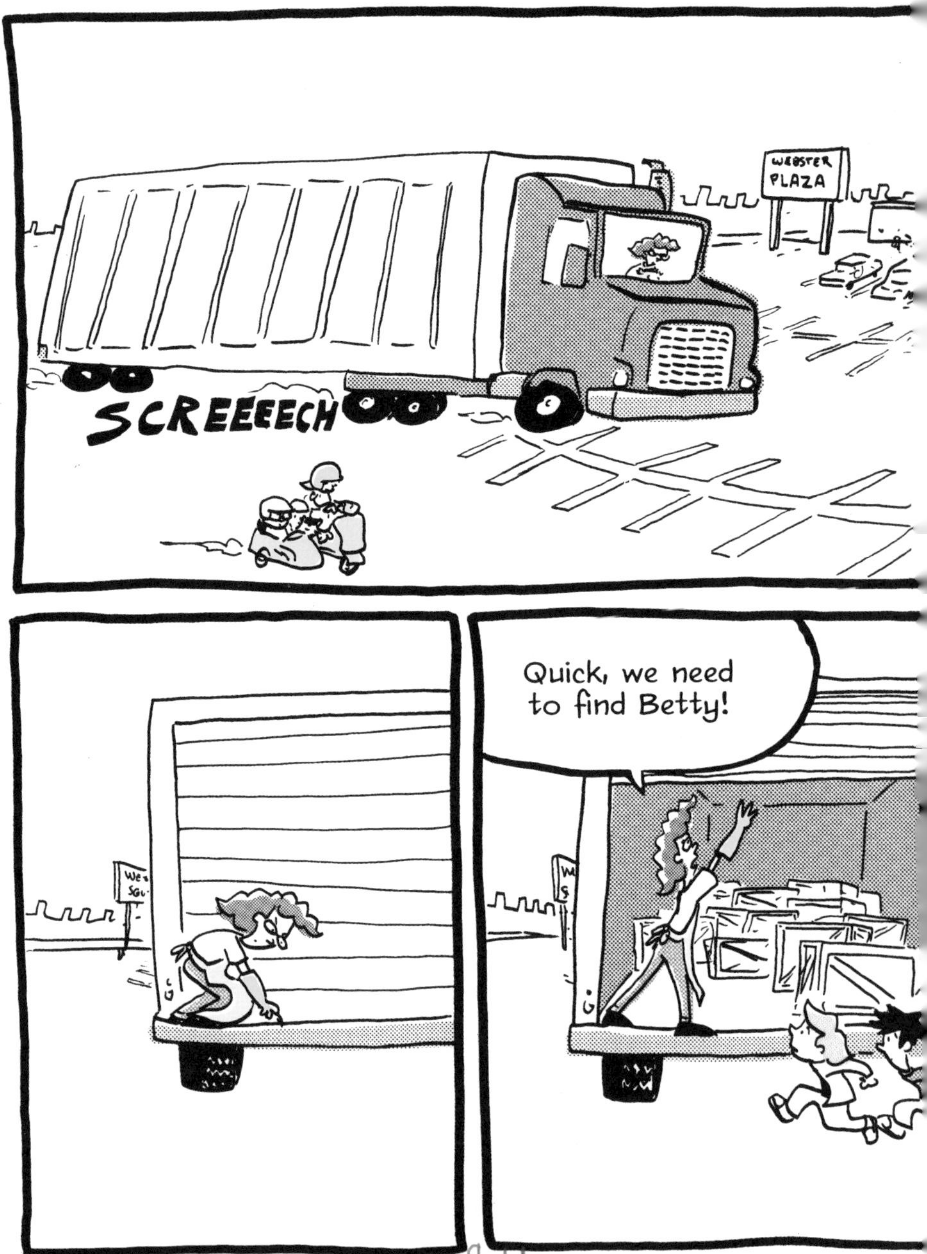
WEBSTER
PLAZA
SCREEEECH
Quick, we need to find Betty!

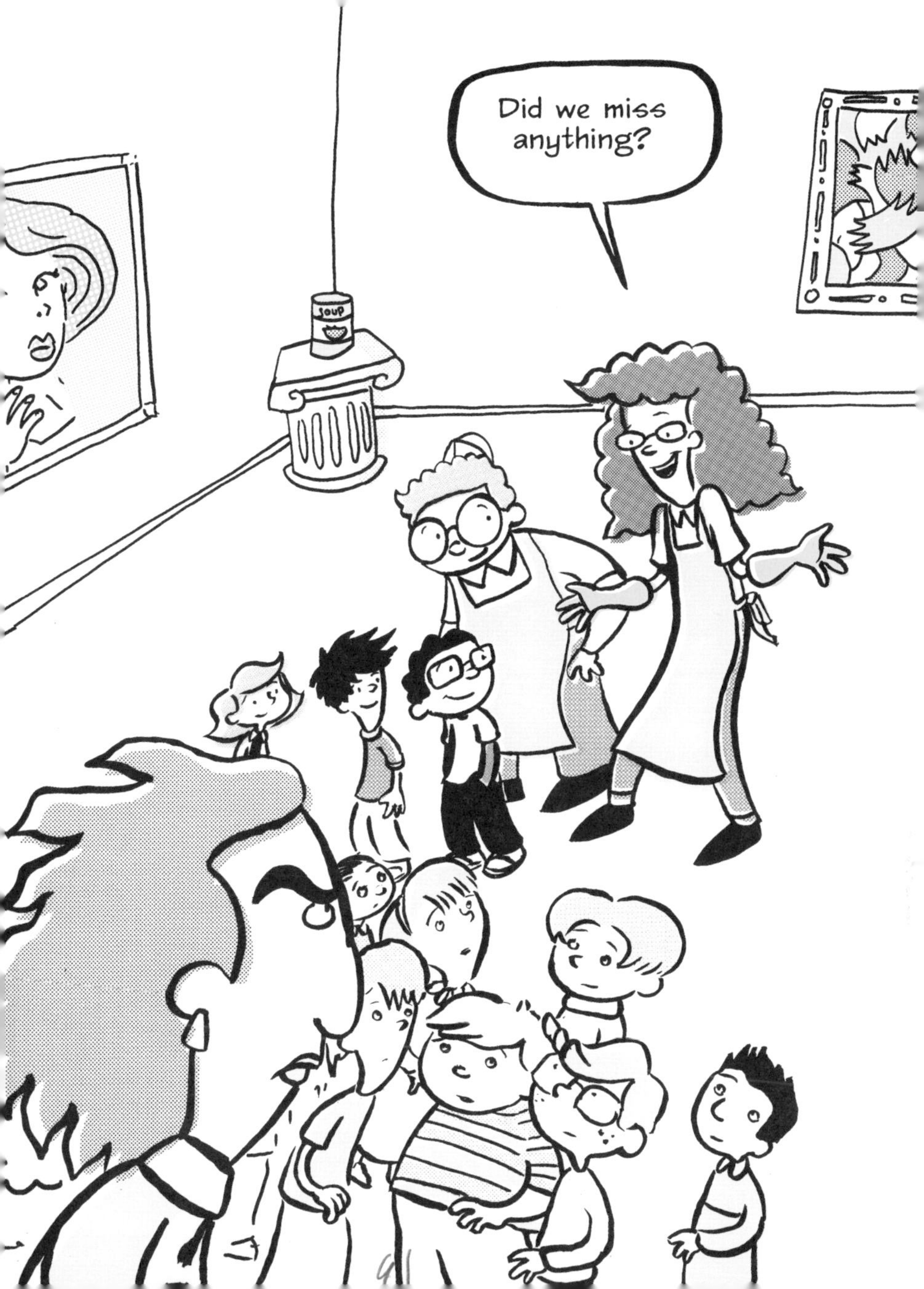
Did we miss anything?
SOUP

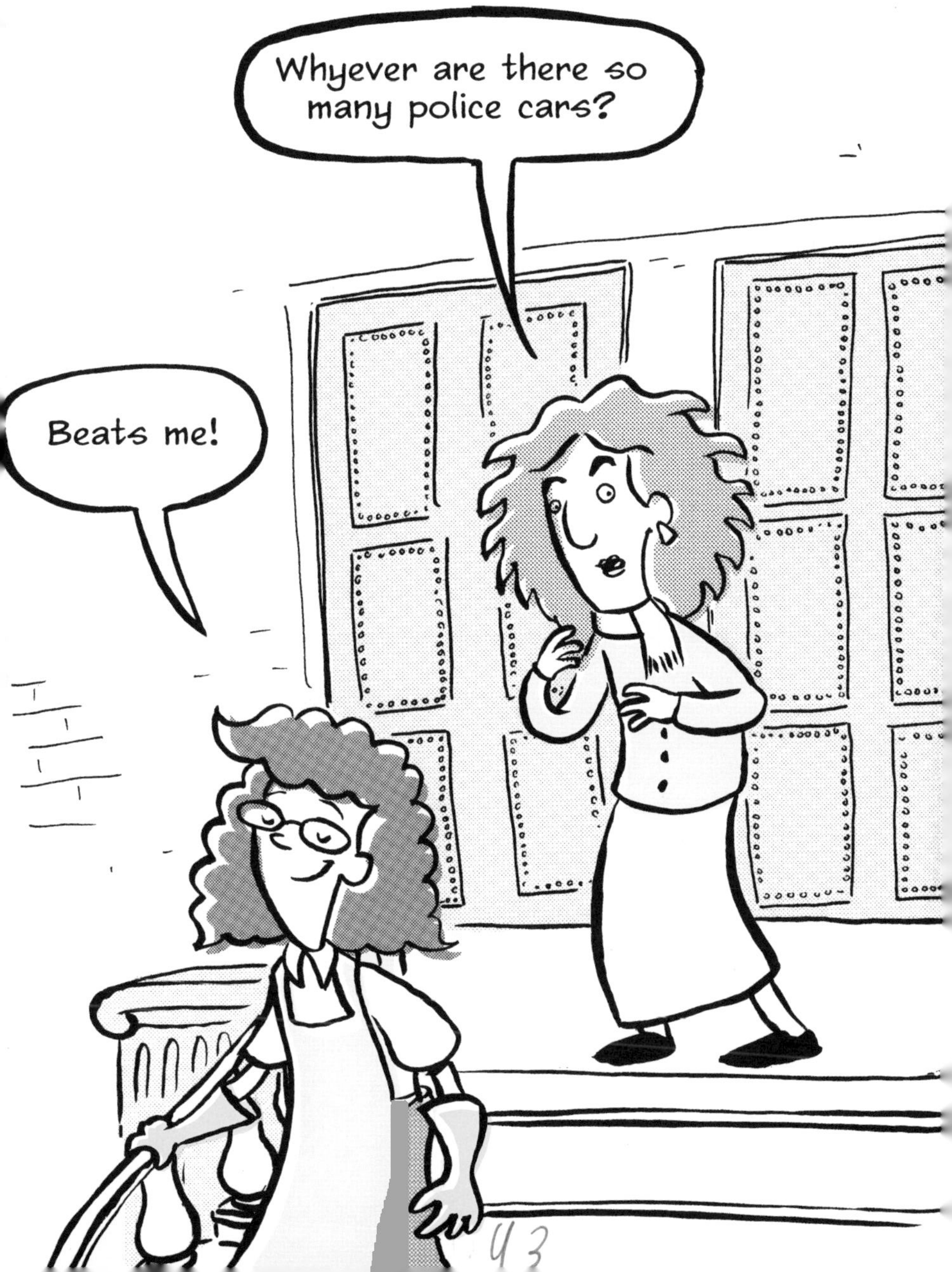
Whyever are there so many police cars?
Beats me!

FOR MARK LYNCH

The author would like to acknowledge the color assist in this book by Joey Weiser and Michele Chidester.

THIS IS A BORZOI BOOK PUBLISHED BY ALFRED A. KNOPF

Visit us on the Web! www.randomhouse.com/kids

Educators and librarians, for a variety of teaching tools,
visit us at www.randomhouse.com/teachers

Library of Congress Cataloging-in-Publication Data
Krosoczka, Jarrett.
Lunch Lady and the field trip fiasco / Jarrett J. Krosoczka.
p. cm.
Summary: Lunch Lady, a secret crime fighter, accompanies the Breakfast Bunch on
a class trip to an art museum, but when Dee, Hector, and Terrence begin to think
there is something strange afoot, she suspects nothing.
ISBN 978-0-375-86730-9 (tr. pbk.) — ISBN 978-0-375-96730-6 (lib. bdg.)
1. Graphic novels. [1. Graphic novels. 2. School field trips—Fiction. 3. Art—Forgeries—Fiction.
4. Mystery and detective stories.] I. Title.
PZ7.7.K76Luf 2011
741.5'973—dc22
2011005907

The text of this book is set in Hedge Backwards.
The illustrations in this book were created using ink on paper and digital coloring.

MANUFACTURED IN MALAYSIA
September 2011
10 9 8 7 6 5 4 3 2 1

First Edition

Random House Children's Books supports the First Amendment and celebrates the right to read.

9 6